Hopes, Dreams and Reality

by
Karen GoatKeeper

Copyright © 2023 by the author.

All rights are reserved, including the right to reproduce this book or any part thereof in any form, except for inclusion of brief quotes.

ISBN-13:

All of the illustrations and text were done by the author.

Sample pages of this book and other books by this author can be found at the author's website: http://www.goatkeeperspress.com.

Other Books by Karen GoatKeeper

<u>Fiction</u>
For Love of Goats
Dora's Story
Capri Capers
Edwina
Running the Roads
Hazel Whitmore Series:
1 Broken Promises
2 Old Promises
3 Mistaken Promises
<u>Picture Book</u>
Waiting For Fairies
<u>Nonfiction</u>
Exploring the Ozark Hills
My Ozark Home
Goat Games
The Pumpkin Project
The City Water Project

Table of Contents

Part One: Storm Warning
Day 1 How Big Is It? — 5
Day 2 Sell? — 15
Day 3 Preparations — 25

Part Two: Stormy Days
Day 4 The Rain Begins — 35
Day 5 Marooned On an Island — 46
Day 6 The Briefcase — 53
Day 7 Enough Rain — 69

Part Three: Facing Reality
Day 8 Flood Waters Recede — 80
Day 9 Learning to Fix Fence — 87
Day 10 Empty Refrigerator — 89
Day 11 Tractor Time — 92
Day 12 Can't Never did Anything — 96
Day 13 Paper Insurance — 102
Day 14 Comparing Dreams — 106
Day 15 Losing Dreams — 109
Day 16 Helicopter Bringing Water — 112
Day 17 Cow Refugees — 118
Day 18 Frustration — 120
Day 19 The Phone: Two-Edged Sword — 123
Day 20 Trouble Is Coming — 127
Day 21 Indecision and Fear — 133
Day 22 Justin — 136
Day 23 New Reality — 148

Epilogue — 151

Author's Notes — 154

Part One

Storm Warning

Day 1 How Big Is It?

"Hey, Mindy. What can I get you today?"

"Hi, Lee. Say, what have you heard about that storm?"

"It's big and headed our way. A lot of flooding and damage comes with it."

"It scares me. You know that creek bottom floods with six inches of rain. Let's make it two sacks of egg crumbles, sunflower seeds, three scratch feed, three range cubes, five oats and two dog food."

"Planning to be flooded in a while?"

"Might as well. Oh, add a mineral block and a goat block." I take some bills out of the bank envelope I'd picked up earlier. A stab of guilt reminds me I cashed the September budget check a week early without asking Justin first. A slip comes out with an account balance on it. I'm close to overdrawn? Justin hadn't transferred money into the checking account yet. Not like him. I'd ask him about it tonight.

"Maybe that storm will miss us," comments Lee as he hands me my change.

"We can hope. Either way, I'll use the feed."

We go out to the room stacked with various feeds. Lee loads mine into the back of my pickup. "Stay safe out there."

"Justin's due in tonight. Maybe he'll stay until after."

"He'll have to, if it floods. You shouldn't be out there alone."

"Suppose so. I like being out there. No nosy neighbors. See you in a few weeks."

"Morning, Mindy," calls the librarian.

"Morning, Carol," I answer as I sign in to use the computers. Internet at the house stinks so I don't have it and use the library computers.

"People Rescued From Rooftops" "Thousands Without Power" "Record Rainfalls!"

Flooding reports about the Category 5 hurricane turned tropical storm dominate the news. Rain amounts are unreal. I stare at pictures of roads filled with water half way up cars.

Aerial shots show suburbs with house roofs like islands in a lake. My stomach knots.

After reading and answering a few emails, I type in the address for a weather service I like. Today's weather is perfect August weather: hot, dry, scattered showers. Tomorrow is more of the same. It's the ten day outlook that worries me.

That storm is due three days from now bringing lots of rain, ten inches and more for three days. The knot is now a cold lump in my stomach. I'll, we'll be stuck for a couple of weeks. If the storm comes in early, I'll get Justin to myself for two weeks, maybe more, instead of just a day.

I'll need some reading material. "Hey, Carol, can you renew a book for me, if I can't make it in?"

"Sure, Mindy. I'll put it on the calendar."

Three weeks will be six books. I find four on the sale table and check out two feeling a bit guilty as I have a stash at home from a book sale to read. Maybe I'll get a couple of them read too, if I'm stuck that long.

The pile of feed in the pickup bed is reassuring. Hungry, wet livestock is not good. Me being hungry and wet is not good either. On to the market.

Half the town must be in the parking lot. I end up parking way out at the far end. It's not that I don't usually park farther out, just not that far. The local paper lists accidents in town and parking lot ones are common. Someone backs into someone else. No bumper car incidents for me.

Inside the store I dodge other shoppers loading their carts. Shelves look like locusts have been by. It's not that I don't have food at home. There's milk from my goats, eggs from my chickens and produce from my garden.

Well, I did have produce. The deer discovered my garden and a four-foot fence is a joke. I'd expected that in the orchard and put up a six-foot fence. Now I'm putting up a six-foot fence around the garden.

There's meat and produce in the freezer. That won't help me if the storm knocks the power out. I scour the store shelves for cans of corn, peas, spinach, fruit and beans. Fresh fruit and vegetables will last a week or so. Potatoes last longer. I snag the last bag of cat food and jug of litter. I definitely don't want to share the house with a hungry cat. It's a different brand from usual so I add some cans of cat food to disguise it. There aren't many of those to choose from either so Sassy will have to get over not having her favorites.

After packing the sacks of groceries in my truck, I head for the gas station glad I filled the tractor tank and brought the diesel can to fill plus an old, dented one. Justin doesn't let me use the tractor much while he's home. He doesn't think I'm big enough and I'm a woman. I do use it when he's off driving a rig cross country.

There's a line as people fill large gas containers, probably to use in generators. We'd talked about getting a generator after the first time the electricity went off. Justin decided not to get one.

The pickup has a full tank and I have the extra cans of diesel in the bed when I leave the station. I go down my mental list and stop at another store to add extra items like batteries, matches and another bag of cat food in case I'm stranded longer than usual. Everything seems covered so I head for home.

The truck rolls down a couple of residential streets with trimmed expanses of grass and some large yard trees trimmed away from the electric lines. Leaving town behind for a paved road lined by grassy, weedy ditches lined by yellow sunflower type flowers, I find I am humming, even singing a few lines of Justin's favorite song. He'll be home tonight.

My last turn takes the truck onto my gravel road. No matter how many times the grader comes by, the gravel is rough. It crunches under the tires. Vibrations jounce me slightly in the seat adding rhythm to my offkey humming. I pass a couple of houses and a road going off toward some hills.

A mile further on the road descends into the creek bottom. Hills line one side of the road. On the other side, flat expanses extend off toward the creek flowing in front of more hills. Where hills end ravines come down to the road and huge culverts run under the road to carry off rainwater. Big, old trees line the road making the road a green tunnel although a few yellow tints are sneaking in now it's mid-August.

The flat expanses were cleared for pasture. A couple of old houses and barns collapsing into the ground mark where families once lived. Some fields are rented out to ranchers wanting to run cattle. These have brush growing up as renters have little incentive to brush hog to keep it out and they stop leasing them when the brush gets too thick. A few are cut for hay and are still nice.

I roll over six culverts before coming to the first of the two by the house. I'm the only one living down here now, seven miles out near the end of the gravel road, ten miles from town. There's a place beyond me, but no one lives there and I've never seen anyone go there. I turn into my driveway revving the engine so the truck pulls up the slope and into the yard, a flat expanse left when the top of a hill was bulldozed off.

Unloading feed comes first. I back up to the barn and turn off the engine. Letting the chickens out to forage on grass trumps even unloading.

"All right, everyone, I'm home. Gate's open." The flock tumbles out of the gate and spreads out across the yard. This bugs Justin, but makes for great eggs.

In the milk room a line of metal trash cans used as feed barrels to thwart the mice holds my weekly feed. Each barrel holds three sacks of feed, but only two oats and one each of the others fit in them now. I'm left with sacks of scratch, cubes, oats and dog food to set in a corner I hope will be out of the way.

Groceries are next. These too overload my storage capacity. Unlike feed sacks, cans are mouse proof. There seems to be a never-ending supply of mice moving into the house, faster than Sassy can catch them. They have too many hiding places.

After changing into work clothes, I head out to the barn to begin evening chores. "Beautiful evening," I tell myself as I pause to take a few deep breaths. "No diesel fumes. No traffic." The sky is clear. The air is cozily warm. A slight breeze is blowing from the southeast. "You'd never think a big storm is coming." I shrug, set down the milk pail and tote in the milk room and get a bucket of range cubes. Each steer gets half a scoop making four scoops.

My eight feeder steers don't need the cubes. They have good grass and put on plenty of weight over the summer. The cubes are an easy way to lure them into the barn and corral.

I walk down the driveway, then a dozen yards down the road and across to the cow pasture gate. By the time I'm in the pasture jog trotting toward the barn, the steers are running over to the barn except for one that targets me, really the bucket. "Don't you dare!" I warn the steer now following close behind me, nose reaching out toward the bucket.

The trick is to race into the open-faced barn at one end and behind the three troughs along the inner wall dribbling the cubes in and getting out the other side before the steers move in. When I buy the steers in the spring, this isn't much of a problem as they are only two hundred fifty to three hundred pounds each. By August they are close to six hundred pounds each with their backs almost to my five foot four height. I do have a stick to wave to keep them at bay, but it's hard to dribble cubes and wave the stick at the same time. I keep moving the troughs out enough to walk behind them, but the steers keep pushing them back.

These steers will be sold in October. I've done this for four years now and made some money at it. I might make more holding them over a year and selling them as meat. Then I would be feeding hay during cold weather and I'm not thrilled with that idea.

Once the steers are busy eating, I walk back into the barn. The steers lick up the last cubes as I look them over. All of them look great. Today I walk back out of the barn on the creek side. "This pasture is awfully low, only a couple of feet above the creek. Those low areas over there hold water in a big storm. And they say this one will be a lot bigger."

The steers are following me toward the creek. Cows are curious about anything new. Besides, I'm still carrying a bucket which must refill magically. I stand looking down into the creek bed toward the creek.

What would happen with ten inches of rain a day for three days? Six inches in one day brings the creek up and lapping at the edges of the pasture. The whole pasture might be underwater. Where would the steers go?

The bucket bangs into me. "Hey, you, it's empty. Back off."

Justin is due in any time, first time in three weeks. I half trot back over to the goat barn for a scoop of scratch feed to entice the chickens back into their coop. It doesn't work on a late town day like today, but it's habit. A few run over to peck up the grain. I will have to come out later to lock their door and yard gate.

My six goats are crossing the bridge into the barn lot when I get back to the barn. I close the barn lot gate behind them. They mob the door to the milk room eager to eat. "Move over," I insist while shoving them aside. "You can't get in until I'm through the door." I squeeze between them and back into the milk room closing the door in their faces.

Glancing around the milk room, everything is in order. I let the first two goats in to run over and jump on their milkstands. It doesn't take long to milk the six, put out some hay and get back in the house.

Justin should be here soon now. I put up the milk, then get out a couple of steaks, his favorite meal. Some fried potatoes and a vegetable will finish out the menu. I baked his favorite cake yesterday. Everything's ready to cook so I sit down and open a book to wait until he gets home.

A couple of chapters later I'm still waiting. Maybe he called when I was at the barn. No message on the answering machine. Maybe he had problems, traffic, a flat tire? I flip on the outside lights as dusk is darkening the yard, race out to lock the chicken's door and gate and back in. I sit down with my book trying to ignore my stomach.

The phone rings when I'm half through the next chapter. Jamming the bookmark in, I drop the book on the table and pounce on the phone. "Hello, Justin? What happened? Where are you?"

"I'm still in St. Louis and won't be coming this time. I guess I should've called earlier. Sorry."

"Nothing happened to you. That's a relief."

"You know about the storm? You should get out of there before it hits."

"I'm staying here. I brought in three weeks worth of feed, groceries. The livestock needs tending. We'll be fine. Oh, I took out the money for September early as I was getting the extra feed and the account is pretty low."

"That place and the livestock are too expensive. All it's good for is work and spending money with no return. And it's a trap in a big storm. Have you seen the forecasts?"

"I saw them today. I'll be safe up on this hill. So will the livestock."

"That place is a real dud, a disaster. The road floods. The electric goes out. No cell service. It's a trap. I want to sell it."

"I don't."

"You could come back on the road with me. I miss my partner. The company pays plenty for team drivers. We could afford a really nice place in four or five years."

"This is a nice place."

"It's a dud. Isolated. Lousy road. I miss you."

"I'm done driving."

"You loved driving. All you need is to get back on the road again."

"No. I want a home and a family. We can't have that if I'm driving."

"There's time for a family in a few years, after we have money. I grew up with hand-me-downs, wondering if I'd eat at night. No child of mine will grow up like that."

"Justin, I'm pushing thirty. A few years from now might be too late."

"That isn't the place. We need to sell it, try again somewhere else. Think about it. We can do a lot better. I'll call tomorrow night about this time. Bye."

"Bye." The phone goes dead. I put it down and sink back into the chair. Sell the place? My body goes numb.

We bought the place five years ago to raise a family, retire from driving. I was tired of driving, always being on the move. It wasn't the first place or even the sixth or seventh we looked at. The pastures were overgrown. The house and barn needed repair. It was old Mrs. Watson's pictures of the place when her husband was alive and able to care for it that got us to buy it, me really.

Fixing the place up took lots of work and money. Justin missed driving and hated being tied down. A family could wait. He went back to driving.

I do get lonely with him on the road so much. No cell service is a bother, but the cordless helps. Sassy and the goats are company. I miss him.

Wiping away some tears, I get up and cook a steak with potatoes and veggies for me. The rest will make dinner tomorrow night. Sassy appears sniffing the aroma of steak.

"You appreciate my cooking. We're on our own for now."

If Justin forces the sale of the place, what will happen to Sassy? My gray cat is my best friend here. He won't allow pets in the cab. That will send her to the shelter and she's not a cute kitten. I shake my head to throw such thoughts away for now and open my book to read over dinner. Sassy lays on my lap accepting small nuggets of steak.

My plate is empty of food and in the way of my book. My knees are stiff from the weight of cat on them. Sassy protests as I push her onto the floor to get up and clean up. That leaves my mind playing over Justin's call.

He said he missed me. I miss him too. He had wanted a family too. Or had he? I wanted to believe he did. He did say to wait. I definitely don't want to go back to driving. What can I do, if the place is sold?

I met Justin when I was a sophomore in college studying ecology. He was the tall, dark and handsome guy: dark brown hair with blue eyes; a big laugh; love of going places and seeing things like parks and museums; a good, exciting job taking him all over the country. We hit it off. I dropped out of college and we got married. I went to driving school and joined him on the road for five years. So now the only skill I have is driving and I don't enjoy it anymore.

Now my home is here. I love it here. I know some people here. I'm happy here.

The dishes done, I want my mind to stop worrying at this mess. I rummage through the shelf of DVDs to pick out a thriller. It starts as I settle into my recliner trying to ignore the empty one beside mine. Sassy makes a beeline for me and is up before I am quite settled. I hug her and let her settle onto my lap. Even the thriller doesn't hide the empty feeling inside.

Day 2 Sell?

"Staying up so late was stupid. Sassy, you slept well, didn't have any worries about being homeless, did you? I need coffee."

I crawl out of bed and get dressed. Time to start the day.

The radio blares: "Storm warnings are in effect for all of central Missouri starting tomorrow night. Anyone in a low-lying area should evacuate. This storm has high winds, dangerous lightning, large amounts of rain. This warning runs for four days. Expect flooding and power outages."

"Tomorrow night? That gives me two days. Milking time."

A few puffy clouds are tinged with pink over the hills behind the creek as I walk toward the barn. Standing on the steps to the milkroom door I turn to look over at them again. Now they are a bright pink against a deep blue sky.

Off in the distance a barred owl calls *Who cooks for you, who cooks for you all?* I smile finding the saying fits the call in syllables, if not in sounds. The air is cool with a hint of autumn. My smile fades as memory kicks in. Can I leave this? Should I leave this? I don't want to.

"All you want to do now is sell. What if I refuse? Is this a choice between the place and you? Please don't make it a choice. There must be a way to keep on as we have been."

Inside the milkroom, I flip on the lights, set the milk pail and tote on the counter and open the oat barrel. Through the door to the barn comes the grunting and moaning sounds Nubian goats make as they sleep. These disappear when the door is opened and two scramble to their feet to charge the door.

Precious and Priscilla are always eager to be first to the grain. They leap onto the milkstands and I put out their food. Fastening the stanchion isn't necessary most of the time, but I do it anyway, just in case. Goats startle easily.

"I know he thinks you are a waste of time and money," I tell Priscilla as I milk her. "I don't. I guess you won't have to worry as he won't be coming back here again. Maybe you should worry. What will happen to you, if he sells the place?"

Precious is half through her feed as I start milking her. "I'm glad to be here. I wanted a home, a family and bugged him until he said he did too. Did he say that just to shut me up? We did save up to buy the place."

I pour the milk into the tote. As the goats are finishing their grain, I run my hands over their sleek backs. Their brown fur is so soft. Precious is a golden brown like my hair. Priscilla is almost blond.

When I open the door to let these two out, four heads vie to get in. Precious shoves these eager goats out of her way and goes out closely followed by Priscilla. That lets Gem and Topaz slide in before the traffic jam locks in again. I put feed in front of them and start milking making sure to start with Gem as she is a vacuum cleaner inhaling her grain.

"Why did I want a place so badly? I guess it's because girls are supposed to want marriage and family. That's what my father told me."

I switch goats. Topaz savors her oats. "Do I really want a family? I do want to stay here. It's so nice to hear the birds instead of engines all the time. You know, Justin loves driving, loves the engines, the roads. He gave them up for this place for two years."

After pouring the milk in the tote, I run my hand down the backs of these goats. Gem is a smoky gray with tiny white diamonds scattered on her sides. Topaz is deep red. As I let them out, I wonder if I could find material or blouses colored like them.

Only two heads crowd the door now. Gem and Topaz slither out between my two black goats. I had a hard time telling Hope and Jewel apart at first. Hope has long black ears edged in brown and Jewel has frosted or white ears and nose and a white cap on her head. These two are slow eaters.

"Morning, Hope. Wish you could tell me what to do. I know what my father would tell me. Give the place up. A good wife stays with her husband doing what he tells her to do."

I switch goats. "Well, Jewel, I don't know if I believe a wife's dreams don't count. My college friends thought that was nuts. I want to be a good wife. I love my husband. But I love it here and you too."

I'd believed animals were just animals until I got the goats and chickens. Each goat has her own personality. They show affection to each other sometimes and to me, especially if I have food.

Milking is done. Chickens are next. "The place is kind of far out. But not that far. And the town's nice. True, there's no cell service and the road floods and it can be a week until it's fixed and the power goes out. I guess you do have a point."

I watch my flock pop out of their door and into their yard. The hens attack the scattered grain. The rooster struts out and crows before calling hens over to where he has found grain for them to eat.

"You show off. Chickens aren't hard to sell, I suppose. I'd be stuck using those pale things from the market. Or I would when I got to cook. I'd have to put all my things back in storage."

Walking back to the barn I see the clouds are blazing white against a pale blue summer sky. The sun has topped the trees over the eastern hills. Sunlight highlights trees on the western hills as it creeps down toward the yard.

Gathering up several flakes of hay, I go out into the main barn to stuff it into the hay trough. The goats run over to check it out. "If Justin makes me sell, where will you go? He'll send you to the sale barn for the meat buyers. How do I send my friends to be goatburger?"

Arlo, my livestock guardian dog, comes over for attention. Together we walk out of the barn and across to the gate leading to the bridge. We walk part way across and I stare down into the ravine.

There are two ravines, one on each side of the house hill. Their deep vee shape goes down at least ten feet. Right now, the ravine is dry. A six-inch rain puts a torrent two or so feet deep pouring down it toward the road culvert. "How much rain would it take to fill this thing up? Arlo, I don't really want to know the answer to that."

We walk back to the barn. The goats are done eating hay. Half is left for later as they head for the door. Browse up in the hill pasture is so much better than hay in their opinion.

I close up the feed barrels and gather up the pail and tote. Milking times can be hectic. Usually, they are a quiet time with a regular routine. I look forward to being with the goats either planning out my day or relaxing at the end of it, the bookends of my day. The milk is an added delicious bonus.

Town is a trip I won't be making until after the storm. There are a couple of people who get milk from me, but not until then. This milk gets strained and refrigerated for cheese in a day or two. After the rain starts and I can't go out.

Justin is right about one thing. There's always something to be built or repaired around the place. "Today's project is finishing the garden fence," I tell myself as I put a handful of oatmeal, some raisins and milk in a bowl. The bowl goes in the microwave for a minute.

My college roommate clued me in on microwave oatmeal. The fancy stuff in the market costs a fortune. This is as good, well, a bit crunchier and a lot cheaper.

The radio news is winding up. "Parts of central Arkansas have broken all time rainfall records with areas receiving twelve inches in the last twenty-four hours. The Arkansas River is approaching flood stage. Flooding and power outages are widespread. The storm continues to move north."

Two days. I have two days to get ready. Justin wants me to leave. Where would I go? There is no place to go. I have feed and food. The house and barn are on a hill. "I'm staying."

After breakfast, I walk out to the garden. Two rolls each a hundred feet long of six foot tall one by two inch welded wire fence lie there. These are heavy, difficult to put up. I stare at them.

"What's the point? If we sell the place, the garden will become a weed patch. All my work on it will be a waste of time."

The orchard next to the garden is surrounded by the same six foot wire. The trees look good. They're several years old and my first crop of Red Delicious are just getting ripe.

"I'm not leaving." I open the first roll of wire and unroll enough to start putting it up. Justin helped with the other fencing and it went up quickly. This will not be fast.

One thing about this wire, it is stiff. Once I get the end of it fastened on the new, tall posts I put in last week, the rest of the wire flips up into place across the front of the garden with little effort on my part.

Getting around the corner is another story. Even with half the roll unrolled, the remainder is heavy, clumsy, infuriating to move around the bend. And the roll is used up half way down the side of the garden.

The second roll is maneuvered into place and unrolled part way. I stand the end up and fasten it to the post where the last roll ended. I use a foot to shove the roll to unroll a little more. Except the ground is sloping down. The roll gathers speed and goes off the edge of the ravine. "Drat. Now what do I do?"

I put up the fencing to almost complete that side of the garden leaving the back not done. And the fencing is down in the ravine tangled in brambles with their multitudes of thorns, curved and sharp, waiting for anything or anyone to go by. "It's lunch time." I walk back to the house.

After lunch, I stare down at the wire. An experimental tug had the expected result. The wire didn't move. There is no way I can roll it back up the slope even if I wanted to brave all those thorns. "Tractor time. I walk over to the tractor shed and back it out.

Backing the tractor down the six foot wide runway behind the orchard and garden, I stop a short way from where the fence goes down into the ravine. We'd left this strip in case the edges eroded in some flood and so we had room to work on the fence without balancing on the ravine edge.

I toss the hooked end of a log chain down over the wire and pull. It pulls up. I try again. And again. It finally catches.

Fastening this to the tractor, I chug down the way. The wire comes up dragging brambles with it.

Turning the tractor off and leaving it sitting there, I walk around the orchard fence, around into the yard and back to where I can push up and fasten the new garden fence. The bramble branches catch my hands as I pull them out of the wire and toss them back into the ravine.

It's late and nearly time for chores before I get done. I leave the wire, release the chain and drive the tractor back to its shed. Next stop is the house to clean up and gather my milking equipment.

For some reason I will never understand, the goats come bouncing in ready to eat their grain without my calling them. Milking goes fast. Even the chickens run back in their pen when I call. I still have daylight left. I put up the rest of the fence. It comes out a few inches short of the orchard fence. I'll tie it together with wire another day.

Sassy hangs around the kitchen as I cook up the second steak. The phone rings as I am putting food on my plate. I pick it up and sit down in my chair. "Justin?"

"Hi, Mindy. I'm headed for L.A. tomorrow, taking I-70 ahead of the storm. Have you seen the reports?"

"They were on the news. Central Arkansas is flooded. It's moving into northern Arkansas."

"I watched it on the motel TV. No clouds there?"

"The sky's clear, the clouds pink tonight. Lovely day."

"You need to get away from that place before it gets there. We need to sell it. Too isolated. Storms strand you. No electricity. No water. Horrible place."

"I have plenty of feed and groceries to last me several weeks. The buildings are up on a hill. I'll be fine. The animals will be fine."

"Reports say cities will be weeks getting power on. That's a small town. You'll be stranded, alone, for who knows how long. We need to sell. I need you with me again."

"I don't want to drive again."

"Why not? You were good. We had lots of fun on layovers. Remember Yellowstone? And Grand Canyon?"

"We did have fun sightseeing."

"You were the one who found the interesting places to go."

"Those are good memories."

"Let's do it again. Get rid of that place. All it does is eat money, time and work. It will never pay for itself. The company needs drivers. We can make lots of money in a couple of years. Find a better place then."

"I like this place. It has lots of possibilities like the feeder cattle."

"And, if you lose one, you lose any profit. If you lose two, you're in the hole. And the house is old and needs repairs. It all takes money. Money you take from me and my driving."

"The place can bring in some money."

"Not enough."

"I suppose not."

"You stay there playing homesteader while I go out working. And you expect me to pay for it? I'm tired of paying for you to stay there playing."

"I'm not playing. You know how much work it takes here."

"Too much. We need to sell. We can see more places, find a better place to buy, a place we both like."

"I'll think about it."

"All we need, really, is a place to crash for a few days. Forget the livestock. It ties you down. We wanted to go places, see things."

"I was tired of always being on the move. I like staying here, the livestock, the routine."

"I've got to go. I'll call you tomorrow night. Bye."

"Bye." The phone is dead in my hand. I set it down on the table. My meal is cold so I reheat it in the microwave and sit down to eat. Sassy gets more than her share of the steak.

Justin is right. I've been using money from his driving to pay for everything on the place. So many things needed fixing, replacing or building after years of neglect. It took money. Money I wasn't earning and didn't have. Well, I did have money stashed from when I drove. I'm using that too, but it won't last forever. Justin keeps the finances and he would know.

If I did start driving again and we kept the place, no one would be here. Things would fall apart again. The animals would have to be sold. What am I to do? If I don't agree to sell, what happens to us? Do I lose Justin? I bury my head in my arms and let the tears fall.

It's the middle of the night when I wake up. My shoulders are stiff. My feet and legs are cold. I stand up teetering, holding onto the edge of the table as I take tentative steps toward the bathroom blinking sleep from my eyes.

I get ready for bed and crawl in under a blanket. August nights are too warm for a blanket, but I'm cold. It's not long before I'm too hot and fling the blanket off. Sleep has fled. My mind is racing: Sell the place. Go back to driving. I don't want to. I need money. Sell the place. Start driving. Don't want to. How do I pay the bills? Sell the place or lose Justin. I love him. Sell the place. What about Sassy? Where will the goats go? Be sensible. Sell the place. I love it here.

To Sassy's disgust, the sheet follows the blanket and I get up. The dinner dishes need washing. What's on the radio? Nothing I want to listen to. Something to turn the mind off.

The dishes done, I grab the blanket, wrap up and settle into my recliner to watch a favorite romantic comedy. My mind relaxes. I wake to the opening music behind the main menu. I crawl back in bed and close my eyes.

Day 3 Preparations

"What time is it?" I reach for my bedside clock then fling off the sheet. I race out to the kitchen turning on the radio and starting the coffeemaker. By the time I'm dressed, the coffee is ready and the news cast has me worried. Already my area has severe storm warnings and flash flood warnings beginning around midnight.

Outside the sky is clear. The sun is gathering strength for another hot August day. This morning I feed and let the chickens out before milking. The goats are awake and blocking the door. I go around into the hay section, grab some hay and take it out to the hay trough. The goats abandon the door to mob it.

Precious and Priscilla leave the hay behind and crowd into the milkroom. They eat fast, faster than I can milk the pair. Let loose they crowd up to the door eager to get back to the hay.

"Gem, Topaz, breakfast time." They look over, hay sticking out of their mouths, look back at the hay, look back at me and come over to the milkroom. Like the others, they gobble faster than usual. At this rate I will have to do them one at a time as they get restless when their dishes are empty.

"Jewel, Hope." They ignore me. I go out and grab Hope. She resists, then surges forward dragging me back to the milkroom door. I can't resist a hundred twenty pound dynamo on four feet. Once on the stand she eats fast. I barely have time to get her milked before her dish is empty.

Jewel is last. She is at the door as the hay is mostly gone now. After milking her, I put out more hay. That distracts everyone while I check Arlo's feeder. It's low so I get a bucket of dog food to put in the hopper.

Precious sees me come out with a bucket. That means food. She runs over. "Scram! Dog food isn't good for you." There are lots of things goats will not eat, contrary to popular myths. Dog food is not on that list. Arlo's feeder is inside a small pen the goats can't get into, but I can reach over to fill the hopper without going inside. The goats haven't figured out how to open the lid to the hopper yet.

By the time my oatmeal is ready, the news is over. I turn the radio off. "The storm is coming. It's big. The road will flood. The hill shouldn't flood so the goats and chickens and I are fine. What about the steers?"

I'm positive that low pasture and the hay field will flood with over ten inches of rain. "I'll have to move the steers. Where? It's got to be the hill pasture."

Steers are not easy to herd from one place to another, if they don't know the way. Since they arrived, these have never been outside of their pasture. "How do I get them into the hill pasture? Now is when I need a good cattle dog to round them up and move them across the road."

I laugh. I can just see myself chasing after these steers. I can't run fast enough. "They are bucket trained. Range cubes to the rescue."

I go to the milkroom to get a bucket of range cubes. Walking down the driveway I come to the road and turn left toward the cow pasture gate crossing over the five-foot diameter culvert pipe where the ravine comes down. I've never seen a flood big enough to fill this pipe. The same goes for the matching culvert on the other side of the hill the house sits on.

The hill pasture drive is another ten or twelve feet down the road. Looking at the gate I debate whether to leave it open or try to open it leading the steers over. It's better to have it open. The goats are sure to notice and might come out on the road. They won't be hard to get back in.

Another twenty feet down the road is the gate to the cow pasture. I swing it open and walk toward the barn. A head lifts to watch me. One steer steps toward the barn. That alerts the others and I arrive at the barn with enough time to toss a few handfuls of cubes in the troughs.

Eight steers stand eying the bucket. The cubes in the troughs were an appetizer. They are ready for the rest of them. I rattle the bucket and walk back out of the barn. Being surrounded by six-hundred-pound steers is not healthy, not because they are mean, but because they are big enough to hurt me without meaning to. A few feet away I rattle the bucket, then dribble some cubes onto the pasture.

The steers stand and stare. They never get cubes in the pasture, only in their troughs. One decides to find out if I really put cubes out in the pasture. Soon all eight are arguing over the cubes.

By this time, I'm half way to the open gate. I rattle the bucket to get the steers' attention and pour out more cubes. This time all come over immediately.

Another round of this and the bucket is half empty. The steers are now following me to the open gate. This too is new, so they stop to investigate the gate, the gate posts and stare up and down the road.

I wait out on the road. The steers are half out of the gateway still checking out the road. When I rattle the bucket, one steps out onto the road. Soon all of them are following me across to the drive going up into the hill pasture. I put out half the remaining cubes on the drive in a line leading up to the gate. The steers gobble them up and look into the pasture.

When I walk up into the pasture to pour out the remaining cubes, the steers follow looking all around, but wanting the cubes. Suddenly the goats followed by Arlo burst out of the woods above the hill pasture and streak toward the bridge. Eight heads jerk up. Eight steers spin around and bolt back out of the gate, across the road and into their pasture.

I walk down the drive and across the road. The steers are standing in the middle of their pasture staring toward the gate. No use trying to get them back now, I tell myself. Maybe later. I leave the gate open, walk back up the road and into the hill pasture.

I close the gate to the bridge. Crossing the bridge, I close the barn lot gate. The goats can stay in their barn lot the rest of the day. They are standing in the barn looking out the door and snorting at me.

In hopes the steers would try again, I take another bucket of cubes out and pour a line of them from the cow pasture gate, down the road and up into the hill pasture.

When I look back, one steer has come over to the gate and is reaching his head out to lick up some of the cubes without stepping onto the road. They have amazing tongues, big, thick and long.

"Did I put up all my fencing tools?" I check around the new fence admiring it. "Take that, you pesky deer. You got my tomatoes and my peppers. But I'll have fresh lettuce and spinach."

The log chain is still by the fence. I pick it up and head over to the tractor shed. The chain goes back on its hook. I close the doors. The implements are under a sloped roof along the side of the workshop. They should be all right. All the tools are back in the workshop and the door is closed.

"All of this should be fine. I looked over the barn this morning and it's fine. The chicken house is secure. I guess we're ready for the storm."

I go in the house, make a sandwich and come out to check on the steers. When I walk down the driveway to the road, I can see the steers on their way up into the hill pasture gobbling and arguing over the line of cubes. I stand watching, eating my sandwich.

Popping the last bite in my mouth, I walk down the road and up to the hill pasture. The steers are exploring this new pasture. I close the gate resisting the urge to cheer which will probably spook them.

Walking over to the cow pasture, I go to the barn. If it floods, the hay stored in the back section will be ruined along with any plans to hold the steers over the winter or sell it. This is an old barn with a three-foot-tall concrete foundation around it with another wall separating the hay and animal sections. A cement ramp goes up a foot to the hay section door and is normally high enough to keep flood waters out.

"Those storm pictures showed water more than a foot deep. How can I block this off? The door shuts tight except for this bottom. Wood will wash away. I need something solid and soft. Like sand? Sandbags? Where do I get sandbags?"

I've seen pictures of people filling sandbags to put on top of levees. They're just bags of sand tied shut. "I've got plenty of empty feed bags and hay twine. There's sand by the creek."

I jog back to the barn for some sacks, six should be enough, twine to tie them closed, a spade and the tractor. I laugh carrying the spade. I remember being so embarrassed at the feed store one day shortly after moving here calling the pointed tool a shovel, when a shovel has a flat end. That mistake marked me as city. I pile my supplies on the platform over the forks, start the engine and head for the cow pasture.

There is a gate to the creek on the far side of the cow pasture. The sand pockets shift with every high water event or small flood. I scout around and spot one, a bigger one, put the tractor in neutral next to it, turn off the engine and get down.

Shoveling sand is hard work, slow work. Sand is powdered rock and heavy. I half fill a sack. "Maybe I should put this up. Oof! This is heavy. New plan."

Changing tactics, I fill a sack a third full, set it on the bed. The next sack is poured into the first one which I tie off. Once the six are tied closed, I put the spade across between them. The tractor chugs its way back across the pasture to the barn.

Backing the tractor up to the hay section door, I only have to roll each sand bag off and into position. I move the tractor every couple of bags. The six close off the space under the door.

The front of the barn opens into two pens to make loading and unloading the steers in and out of trailers easier. I secure all the gates. The feed troughs might wash away or get broken. I load them on the tractor to take to the house. Simple as these things look, just a trough on legs, they are expensive. "That's all I can do here. I'll be back to clean up after the rain."

Once more I see that the tractor is back in its shed with the door closed. The spade is put away. The hay troughs are balanced on the implements until they can go back to the cow barn.

When I go out for chores and milking, a south wind is blowing across the yard rolling anything loose in its path. The trees are swaying. A rushing roaring sound surrounds me warning of more to come.

The goats are still disgusted. They didn't get to eat all they wanted in the pasture and mob the milkroom door. I put out extra hay to distract them.

When I go across to call the chickens, mare's tails are blowing across the sky. These high icy clouds usually come before and after storms. They blaze vivid white over lower clouds coloring in the sunset.

While milking the goats, I go over my preparations. I can't think of anything else I can do except wait. Justin was very right. I'm looking at days or a week sitting here while the storm goes by washing out the road. Then I wait days for the road department crew to come out with the grader. The electric crew follows them.

Listening during dinner I hear the radio blare out weather warnings. The commentators natter on. Hurricanes are supposed to weaken once they get over land, then blow themselves out moving northeast as tropical storms, not move almost straight north and get up to the Ozarks. This one had weakened to a tropical storm. It hadn't blown itself out. It hadn't moved northeast.

My area is still under warnings. The counties on the southern border are under watches which means the storm has started for them. At most I have six hours before the rain starts.

My rain gauge only holds eight inches. That's been plenty for all the storms I've watched come through before. Most big storms only dumped four to five inches in a day. An occasional one dropped six. I set out a five-gallon plastic bucket as a rain gauge, putting rocks around it to foil the wind.

After dinner, I walk out to lock up the chickens. A few pockets of stars still dot the sky. Most of the sky is dark. My stomach clenches around dinner leaving a cold knot inside.

"You're in for it now, girl. Too late to cut and run." I walk back in the house to hunt for an engrossing movie to distract me.

The phone is ringing as I get back inside. I race into the kitchen and grab it. "Hello?"

"I was about to hang up. Isn't the message part working?"

"It doesn't kick in for five rings. Where are you?"

"Middle of Kansas. Has the storm started?"

"Not yet. It's windy. The sky is clouding over."

"I wish you'd gotten out of there."

"There's no place to move the animals. And the warnings are for the whole area. We should be fine up on the hills here."

"We should find a place in California. Lots of sunshine. No floods."

"Wildfires. Droughts. Earthquakes. Expensive. This place is fine."

"All we need is a little house to stay in from time to time. Someplace without all the work."

"What's that noise? Do I hear a dog?"

"The company saddled me with this new driver as a team. They are really pushing for driving teams to speed up deliveries. Her dog yaps and gets in the way. It's driving me crazy."

"You never did want pets in the cab."

"I wish you were my partner again. We made a good team. I really want to sell that dud of a place, get away from all those headaches."

"I don't want to drive again. And this isn't such a bad place. I like it here."

"Especially if someone else pays the bills while you play homesteader. I'm done paying your bills. Get that dog away from me!"

Mindy listens to Justin and this new driver square off about her dog.

"I've got to go. I'll call tomorrow night. Bye."

"Bye." I hang up. He still wants, insists on selling. There will be no more money coming in. And I'm to go on the road again, want to or not.

"Sassy, do you think I'm playing at homesteading? I don't. Look at that fence I put up. And those sandbags. You need to tell him I'm trying to make some money. It's not my fault there are so many repairs needed. It's not my fault there's not enough pasture for more steers." My stomach hurts as I go hunting for a movie.

"Tonight, I wish I could watch the weather channel," I mumble as I turn on the DVD player and put a disk in. We'd opted to save the money for satellite TV and just watch movies. Now I'm glad we don't have that monthly bill. "Not that watching the storm coming in changes anything."

Halfway through the movie the room lights up then trembles from a clap of thunder that almost bounces me onto the floor and sends Sassy racing for the bedroom closet. Afterwards a steady pounding on the roof makes it hard to hear the dialog. I walk over to the window. Lightning backlights the clouds throwing their jagged, rounded shapes into momentary sharp relief. A curtain of rain glistens in pulses matching the lightning outside the window. The rumble of thunder ebbs and flows, loud and soft, with the rushing of the wind underneath. "It's here. We're in for it now."

The movie plays on. I'm watching the rain lit up by the lightning flashes. The drops are large. A sheet of water covers the ground. I'm alone surrounded by the drumming of the rain on the roof, rat-a-tatting against the windows, the roll of thunder and the rush of the wind. It drowns out the movie. It drowns out the turmoil in my head. It scares me. It fascinates me. It lulls me to sleep later in my bed curled up with Sassy.

Part Two

Stormy Days

Day 4 The Rain Begins

"Why am I awake in the middle of the night?" I grope for my clock. "Six thirty! Where's the daylight?" Dark grey windows pretend morning has arrived.

Rain drums on the roof with occasional swishes saying the wind is still blowing. I slide out from under the sheet leaving Sassy still curled up, pull on my clothes, then head for the kitchen to make coffee. Rain is blowing against the window.

The coffeemaker is working. The radio is on reporting ten inches of rain overnight in St. Louis. Strong winds have toppled trees breaking power lines throughout the area. Low lying areas are flooded. You are asked to stay home. If you must drive, don't drive into moving water. Storm warnings are in effect for the next three days.

I stare out the window. The screen is so covered with water, the yard is blurry, dark as late evening. "St. Louis got ten inches. How much here?"

Sipping on hot coffee I start putting on my rain gear. Tall rubber boots. Rain slicker. Where's my umbrella?

Carrying my milking equipment and balancing the umbrella, I open the door to step out onto the mud porch. The room is cool and loud with the sound of the rain. When I open the door to the porch, wind yanks the screen door, showering me with mist.

Wind roars through the trees sounding like a major highway. Leaves and twigs litter the yard being pushed into wavy dams by the water flowing down. A steady rush underpins the drumming and roaring.

Pushing open the screen door, I stick the umbrella out and push the button. It springs open and swivels as the wind turns it into a kite. I force it back pointing into the wind, stepping out into a yard now covered with half an inch of water moving down toward the road. The rushing sound gets louder as I approach the barn.

Inside the milk room I relax in dry and still. After setting the pail and tote down, I go out into the barn. The goats are gathered up at one end. I follow the rushing sound out the door again fighting the wind with the umbrella. The ravine is a third full of rushing water. A small branch rides down brown, foamy waves heading for the culvert.

"Well, we've gotten over six inches. And it's adding up fast with this downpour. Inside day for everyone."

Precious has crept down to the door to see what I am up to. When I start to enter the barn again, she spooks as do the others right behind her. "You sillies. It's an umbrella, a portable roof." I laugh at my big, bold Nubians so convinced the umbrella is a monster coming to get them, close it and go back into the milk room.

The chickens are sitting on their roost or standing around when I open the door to dump feed in their feeder. "You'll need water. You are stuck inside until after the rain." I go out in the yard to get the water fount. It's easy to fill from the downspout over the rain barrel. I set it in the house. A hen immediately kicks dirt in it.

"I can see this won't work. What can I set it on?" Closing the door, I head for the workshop to find a chunk of wood. "Wait, I have those stones I didn't use for the garden entrance." A couple of these fit under the water fount, now cleaned out again.

Even with the umbrella, I'm getting wet from rain blowing against my legs. I'm glad to get back into the milk room. The goats are glad to come in to eat while I milk.

"Since you are convinced you will melt in the rain, I guess you goats will stay inside today," I tell them later as I stuff their hay trough full of hay. "See you after lunch."

Leaving the milk pail and tote on the porch, I walk down the driveway. The culvert on the goat's side of my hill is a third full. A torrent is pouring down the usually dry wet weather creek running between the cow pasture and the hay field. The ditches along the road are full adding more water. Across the pasture, white foam is racing by so the creek is up to its banks.

A sheet of water pours down the driveway. On the other side water is above the culvert. "What is wrong here?" The reason is obvious when I get near the culvert. A small tree or a big branch is lodged across the pipe with smaller branches sticking out snagging leaves, twigs and other debris to form a dam.

"So much for staying dry." I close and set the umbrella down. Water runs down my neck soaking my shirt and jeans. "Oh, that's cold!"

I edge out to the top of the culvert, trying not to slip in the mud. I stoop down and water foams up around, then into my boots. "Drat. I hate wet feet. Oh, well. Too late now." I grab a branch and pull.

The branch slides out and I toss it to the other side of the road. It slips off the other end of the culvert and disappears. I grab another branch. It won't budge. I try another until there are no more not part of the tree. Some water starts flowing through the culvert dropping the level on the road.

"Can't leave that or the yard will flood. Can't pull it out. Maybe I can cut off those small branches so it goes on through." I go to get my bow saw, my best friend when I check fences for fallen limbs. It's bow shape makes it easy to carry and use. Its big teeth lining the blade where a bowstring would be cut through wood fast. I stop on the way to dump water out of my boots and lighten the load on my feet. I may be soaked, but I carry the umbrella anyway to keep the rain out of my eyes for now.

Up in the tool room, I oil the saw. Damp saws don't cut well. Back at the culvert, I set the umbrella down again. Water drips into my eyes from my wet hair. I position myself above the small tree and grab the first branch.

The saw bites in and through. I toss it across the road and start on the next one. Three more and the tree swivels into the culvert as I hang onto my saw dragging it out of the almost cut branch before it leaves with the tree. I hear branches scrape along inside the culvert.

As the tree slips out of the culvert to be carried down along with water headed to the creek, debris follows it. The water level in the ravine drops to the same as in the other one and no longer flows across the road. "So much for that."

I dump water out of my boots, retrieve my umbrella, walk down the drive and onto the road. Beyond the torrent in its belt of trees lies my hay field. The crew I hire was supposed to cut and bale it next week, the second cutting I usually sell. Like in the cow pasture, I see standing water in low places. And the creek is visible as a thin line at the far side. If the grass survives as standing plants, the field will be too wet for tractors and baling equipment for a month at least.

"I guess I won't be selling any hay this year." I turn to walk back up the driveway to the house. The sound of an approaching vehicle stops me. I wait.

An SUV marked U.S. Mail pulls over to where I'm waiting. "Mindy, you are wet, girl. You need a new umbrella."

"Had to clear the culvert. I guess you won't be coming for the next few days as the road will flood before tonight."

"There's already a lot of water on it. I'll hold your mail at the post office. Will you be okay down here?"

"I have plenty of food and feed. The hill shouldn't flood. You stay safe. See you after."

Balancing the umbrella, the mail and the bow saw, I walk up the driveway, my feet squelching at every step, so LeAnne can turn around. I wish she could stay and talk for a few minutes as it will be days before I talk to anyone except by phone. A lump sits in my chest as I watch her SUV disappear toward town. Fighting the wind, I walk up to the house wishing Justin were here. "I guess he won't be coming back at all except to sell the place. I miss him. And I'm not playing around down here and he knows it."

The bow saw is wiped off and set on the porch in case I need to use it again. The umbrella is propped and draining water onto the cement. Gusts of wind blow rain through the screen and onto the porch. Black clouds keep the day dark.

"How much rain so far? I should check the bucket." I grab the umbrella and go out to the bucket. "Seven inches. I thought as much considering the ravine looked like it did with those other big storms." I empty the bucket and set it up again.

Going through the porch, I step into the mud porch to leave my boots. I'd asked Mrs. Watson about this small room when we looked the house over. New houses don't bother with this great idea. Muddy boots, even wet clothes can be left here and not track up the house.

Back inside, I walk to the kitchen surrounded by the sound of rain drumming on the roof, a steady low pulse of sound accented by swishes. Leaving a water trail, I set down the milk tote and pail as I head for the bathroom. My dripping clothes are dropped into the clothes basket. Maybe I should move it into the mud room until after the storm.

After a warm shower, clean clothes make me feel good except for a grumpy stomach. I head for the kitchen to put up the milk. Cold milk goes into a pot for mozzarella cheese as day old milk works better than fresh. While the milk warms, I make late breakfast while listening to some news talk show. Somehow the rain now leaving me stranded makes politics seem unimportant, part of a foreign world.

After adding rennet to the warm milk to set the cheese, I have half an hour to eat. "The power will probably go out. I'm lucky it hasn't already. No electricity means no pump and no water. I better start filling containers with water."

I spend the next few hours attending to the mozzarella and filling every clean container with a lid with water. There are rain barrels at every corner of the house and barn to use for water for the animals and flushing the toilet. We found them a necessity after the first time the electric went out. Next, I make sure to have candles ready for light.

Our first year here, Justin and I would go to farm auctions. Auctions are as much social gatherings as sales and we met a lot of people. But we started piling up boxes of things we had no use for, so we quit going. We did buy some of our tractor implements and a wide assortment of stuff including a big box of candles at ones we went to. Later I bought a box with a dozen candle holders in it. After a few candlelight dinners, the box got shoved into a corner until the first time the power went out. Now I'm glad to have them just in case.

The cheese is cooling in its mold. The filled containers are stashed in various places. The animals should be checked on as the goats will need more hay.

Outside the roar from the ravines is louder, or so it seems. The wind has dropped to a stiff breeze. I go to the goat barn first and put out more hay. I have to clean some soggy hay out of their water basin hooked to a hose attached to a special never freeze faucet next to the barn. The goats are not happy, but enjoy getting fresh hay.

The water level in the ravine is creeping higher. I go out and walk down to check the culvert. It doesn't appear to be clogged. It's half full. The road ditches are overflowing onto the road.

The driveway, now a shallow creek, has a series of small ruts being eroded into the surface. "I'll need a truckload of gravel to repair this mess," I mumble cringing at yet another bill. Looking across to the cow pasture and hay field, I can see flowing water along the creek edges.

The other culvert is half full like the other one. Water from the ditches stretches almost across the road here. Water flows along the creek side of the hay field.

Huddled under my umbrella I trudge back to the house, shivering a bit from the damp air. There's nothing I can do until the rain stops. Sassy curls up on my lap for an afternoon I spend immersed in a book, a thriller to distract me from the rain.

"Time to get up, Sassy. Chore time. Come on, wake up." I dump Sassy onto the floor, set my book aside and stand up. Sounds of rain accompany me as I gather up my chore equipment.

On the mud porch, I shrug into the damp rain slicker, slip my feet into my muddy boots, grab the milk pail, egg bucket and tote. On the porch I grab the umbrella only to find I can't hold on to everything. "Chickens first."

The chickens are mostly sitting around on their roosts. Some are down eating. A few are perched on or sitting in the nests. "Sorry, group." I shake the last feed down to the bottom of the feeder. "I'll bring some extra feed shortly." Eggs go into the bucket and I head back to the house.

After setting the egg bucket down in the mud porch, I grab things to go to the goat barn. Light spray comes through the umbrella to mist my face. The boots accumulate another layer of mud.

The goats are out of hay. No surprise. I put out more. Tonight, I let in one at a time for grain and milking. I've never seen them eat so fast. I take a couple more scoops of feed over to the chickens, the scoops of grain I would have scattered in the yard. I'm back to the house in record time.

"Maybe I should walk around and see what's going on. Maybe not. It's too depressing. Well, I should find out how much water is in the bucket."

It hasn't been twenty-four hours since the rain began and there's another eight inches in the bucket. "Added to the seven this morning, that's fifteen inches today. Wish the ten inch forecast was right." I empty the bucket, set it up again and walk down the yard so I can check the ravines and road.

There is no road. There is a creek where the road is supposed to be. Down the road toward town just beyond the end of the hay field, a big tree lies across the road. Until it's cleared, I'm stranded here, unless I want to walk the ten miles into town.

The real creek is now a small river and half way across my fields. There may be trees down along the creek too. The wind and rain are taking their toll.

The ravines are a bit over half full. I stare back toward the house and barn. The goats, chickens and I are trapped on this hill. There is no way off. And the rain is coming down as steady as ever. I'm cold inside.

Dinner tonight is comfort food, macaroni and cheese. Usually I add some diced onions, but tonight I'm numb. "What do I do if the hill floods? Sassy, we're in trouble. They'd come rescue me, but not the rest of you. What do I do?"

The macaroni sits cooling on my plate. I'm holding Sassy, petting her. She lets me for a long time before struggling to get loose. I reheat the macaroni and eat, swallowing around a cold lump in my throat.

The phone rings. It has to be Justin. I can't tell him. He'd only tell me I was a fool not to leave before the storm. Maybe I was. I take a deep breath as I pick up the phone. "Justin?"

"I saw the weather and wanted to check on you. It's raining?"

"Started last night. We've had fifteen inches so far."

"Then you're flooded in."

"Yes. The ravines are half full. I had to clear one of the culverts this morning. A small tree was caught in it."

"And the road is flooded. And you're stuck for who knows how long. That place is terrible. We need to sell it. Find a better one."

"Yes, the road is flooded. And the creek. And the pastures. Some trees are down because of the wind."

"Are you all right?"

"I'm fine. The steers are in the hill pasture, so they're safe. The chickens and goats are locked up. I stay in the house mostly."

"What's the forecast for there? Have you heard?"

"The storm warnings are for another two to three days. I assume that means rain for another few days. Oh, St. Louis is flooded, ten inches as of this morning. I hope your truck is safe."

"It's in a parking garage, a couple of floors up."

"That's like here. The house is a floor up from the creek so it's okay."

"Team driving is the way to go. We're in Utah now ready to change to I-16. I need a good partner again."

"The dog is a problem?"

"I'm ready to run over the thing. Pets don't mix with driving."

"You'll make it, dog and all. Maybe you can find a new partner out west."

"You're the best partner. I mean it. After this, I'll go back, we'll sell the place and you can join me driving again."

"I don't want to drive again.

"You would once you got started again."

"I don't think so."

"We've never been in the Rockies. We could go there on a layover."

"Maybe."

"I saw a magazine about this guy going to all the national parks. We could do that. You'd like that."

"Maybe."

"Driving's a lot better than all that grunt work repairing buildings and fences that just fall apart again."

"The barn roof isn't leaking."

"It better not after all the time and money we put into it."

"When will you get to LA?"

"Late tomorrow, I think."

"Justin, can you hear me? There's static on the line."

"Barely. What's going on? I'll be..."

"Justin? Justin? Are you there?" Nothing, not even static. I press the button trying to get a dial tone. Nothing. No static. Nothing. The phone lines are buried along the road. The storm shouldn't bother them. The phone's still dead.

"We can't call for help now, Sassy. The phone is dead. I'm surprised the electricity is still on." I walk to the window to stare out at the darkness. I am alone. For the first time in my life, I am totally on my own.

Even in college, my parents came to visit or I went home every weekend. They were a phone call away. Justin might be gone days or weeks at a time, but he always came back, or he did. And he called every night. Now there is no way to call anyone, no one to come and I can't get out. Whatever happens, it's up to me and only me.

I barely notice the sound of rain on the roof now. It's a constant background like the refrigerator. I know water is flowing down the yard, the drainpipes are pouring out water. There is a faint steady roar from the water in the ravine. And the animals and I are here on this hill, all alone.

I start a movie, turn it off. Next, I try reading, but don't get even a page read. I go in the kitchen to start cleaning shelves. Every box and can comes out of the cupboards, gets wiped off and put back after the shelf is wiped clean. It will seem strange to have no dust on things, but I keep at it until I'm tired enough to go to bed. I'll finish in the morning.

Day 5 Marooned On an Island

"Nothing's changed," I tell Sassy in the morning. "Same grey sky. Same wind. Same rain. How much more? Maybe the barn is flooding. I better get up."

On the way to the kitchen, I pick up the phone. It's still dead. The lights and coffee maker still work. I still have water.

My first stop is the bucket. Another eight inches since last evening. That makes twenty-three inches. I dump it and set it up again. The roar is even louder.

"Morning, girls," I call as I walk in the milk room. I drop off the pail and tote before going into the hay section to take the first load of hay out to the goats. I find them still lying around. Topaz continues snoring while the others scramble up to mob the hay trough.

"One at a time. Priscilla, you first." I almost finish milking by the time she is done eating her grain.

"Out, Priscilla. Precious, you're next." I'm wondering if I can milk any faster. She is done and shifting around before I'm done.

Topaz is still snoring when I put Precious out. It's amazing to see her completely oblivious to all the activity going on around her. "Gem, breakfast." I haven't a chance of milking fast enough with this one.

"Out, Gem. Topaz?" No response. "Hope?"

Hope is delighted to get in next. I actually manage to get done milking at the same time she is done eating. I trade her for Jewel. Jewel is back to savoring her grain so I'm done milking before she's done. I go to their door and look into the barn.

Topaz has her head up swinging it back and forth. She reminds me of when I stay up too late and try to get up on time. Her head snaps over to me. She is on her feet and to the door shoving me aside as she pushes through.

Jewel is done, so I put her out while Topaz stomps and surges forward through the stanchion boards. She tries to start eating before I get her dish down in front of her. "Stop it! You'll make me drop it." Somehow the dish gets put down without spilling. No way I am going to finish milking before this goat is done eating.

The chickens complain loudly when I open the door to their house. "I know. It's crowded. The rain will stop someday so you can go out again." They continue to complain until feed is dumped into their feeder. Food makes everything right in their world.

Opening the water fount, I hold it under the downspout. In thirty seconds, it has plenty of water in it. I put the top back on and put it back in the house. "This sure beats using the faucet. See you hens later."

It's easy to walk around the chicken yard to the ravine on this side of the yard. At least, it should be. The ravine is two thirds full. The edges have places where dirt has dropped down into the flood going by. Muddy water with mounds of light brown foam speed down toward the culvert. A couple of the trees on the other slope are leaning out across the ravine. I'm positive they weren't that way before.

Walking down the yard toward the culvert I have to detour around a tree now spanning the ravine. Some of its branches go down into the flood and are catching lots of debris like leaves and smaller branches. This is a disaster waiting to descend to the culvert or it will dam up the ravine and flood the yard and there is nothing I can do to stop it. I am not about to shinny out that tree trunk to cut those branches off.

"Looks like I'm marooned on an island now."

The road turned creek is now a small river. The real creek has broadened across the fields. In low places only the berm pushed up by the road grader along the road separate the two. Fence posts lean at crazy angles depending on which way the water is pushing them, towards or away from the creek.

Most of the fence posts at the end of the hay field seem to be missing. It took us weeks to put those fences up. I think I see the gates still standing.

"Looks like I'll be fencing by myself after the water leaves. Either that or sell and let someone else do the work. It was hard enough for two of us."

The driveway now has big ruts cut into it by the water racing past on the road. Water streams down from the yard. The water isn't deep up in the yard, but it's several inches deep on the driveway.

Walking up beside the ravine toward the barn lot I see a tree is leaning toward the fence and expect it to flatten this fence in another day as the water undercuts its roots. Once the rain is over, the goats will enjoy the leaves. The bridge is still above the flood. I suppose I could walk across to the hill pasture to check on the steers, but that racing, muddy torrent gives me the willies.

Passing the barn, I walk up toward the far end of the yard. Water is pouring down the single huge ravine coming down between two hills and splitting to form the ones on either side of the yard. It curls into breakers on the four to five feet of bluff rock forming the point of the yard. The boulders, broken off the bluff when it was bulldozed, cascade down the slope forming eddies in the current. If the water gets over this bluff, the entire yard will flood.

I take the milk into the house, put it up and eat breakfast. The big news is still the storm. Everywhere from Springfield to St. Louis is setting rainfall records. "Power's out all over. Why not here? Maybe I'll get clothes washed and dried just in case."

My area is still under storm warnings and flash flood warnings. "No joke. Well, Sassy, we're stuck inside again." After putting a load in the washer, I settle into my recliner, Sassy curled up on my lap, to read.

A little after noon I finish the book. Sassy jumps down as I shift to get up and find another one to read later. After giving the goats more hay and eating lunch, I move clothes into the dryer and put another load of muddy clothes in the washer, then go back to cleaning the kitchen. I always enjoyed being in the kitchen growing up. My mother loved to cook, especially soups and stews.

Kitchen time was my time with my mother. We learned to knead and bake breads. I miss her. Driving with Justin, we never seemed to have time to visit and there was no place for them to visit with us.

That is the one disadvantage of this property, for me. My family is in New York and not able to visit Missouri. If I move, maybe I'll move to New York. Except I don't want to move. Maybe I should call them. Maybe I should have called years ago, tried to make peace with my father who despises Justin. What can I tell them except it's raining and I'm stranded? The phone is still dead so I'll call after it gets fixed.

It doesn't take long to do the last couple of cupboards. It's a waste of time to mop the floor as, even leaving my boots in the mud room, my jeans drip water and mud.

The front room is next and full of memories. Justin protested when I bought vinyl flooring for the room. He loved the hardwood flooring and thought he would refinish it. I knew he would never get around to doing it. He complained, but wasn't as unhappy as he pretended. We went on to other projects.

We put new shingles on the roof so it doesn't leak. The barn got new roofing tin so it doesn't leak. The chicken house got rebuilt and the chickens moved in. Justin had never liked eggs much until he tasted these farm fresh ones he's so eager to get rid of.

I painted the inside walls of the house after we decided on a color scheme. We spent hours poring over color sample sheets. He wanted bright colors. I wanted pastels. He got the front room in a warm, glowing yellow and I got the bedroom pastel blue.

I loved seeing the improvements in spite of the work. Justin began finding excuses for going to town. Next came the complaints about the cost. These got louder when I bought the goats. They came to a head when I bought the first steers.

"What do we need cows for?" Justin demanded.

"They're steers, not cows."

"Big deal. They're cows. And we don't need them."

"You want the place to bring in some money and the steers can do that. I'll sell them in the fall."

"If they're still alive. You've already lost one. Will they make back that two hundred? I'm going to St. Louis and hire on a trucking firm there before we go broke out here."

And now Justin wants rid of the place. Should we sell? Can I run the place alone? Do I want to say good-bye to Justin over this? I push that decision out of my mind and attack the dusting with a vengeance.

By milking time, the front room is cleaner than it's been in years. I know it's time to go out, but I sit savoring the feeling of clean, the size of the room, a big sixteen by twenty, and the light look even with the grey, rainy weather outside the windows. It's a welcoming room. It's home.

Outside the rain beats down on my umbrella. The bucket has eight inches in it. "That makes thirty-one inches out of forty-five normal for the year." I dump the bucket and set it up to catch the next day's total.

The chickens are complaining. A couple stick their heads out the door threatening to jump out. Raindrops on their heads change their minds. I shake the feed down in the feeder and am glad the extra I put in this morning has kept the level up enough for today. Eggs and egg bucket go back to the house.

The goats are in the middle of a serious head butting argument. Topaz and Jewel have their hackles up. The dull crunch of their heads hitting makes me cringe. Precious and Priscilla keep interfering, but the argument goes on. Even fresh hay in the trough doesn't distract the combatants.

I start milking. Precious comes in, gobbles her food and shoves her way out the door. Priscilla comes in next. I'm getting faster at milking, but still can't keep up. Gem comes in followed by Hope. That leaves the combatants and they ignore my calls.

I go out to grab Topaz and drag her into the milk room. Jewel sideswipes her. Topaz twists out of my hand to retaliate. I go to get a lead rope.

"It is time to get milked!" I flip the lead rope around Topaz' neck and drag her toward the milk room door. "Jewel, back off." I slap her. She stops to stare at me. I'm in the milk room with Topaz before she can attack again.

Topaz stands on the milk stand snorting. She noses her grain, tosses some on the floor. She stares at the door. I finish milking her.

"You can stand there until Jewel is on the other stand." I grab the lead rope and open the door. Jewel pushes past me snorting. "Oh, no, you don't! Get on that stand. Now!" I shove Jewel toward the stand. She refuses to get up, staring at Topaz.

I resort to putting each front leg up on the stand, shoving Jewel's head through the hole, closing the stanchion and swiveling her back end onto the stand. She stands there snorting, surging back and forth, yelling what must be insults at Topaz. Topaz answers with her own insults. I get Topaz off her stand forcing her to and out the door.

"What got into you two? Stand still. Bored? Thought you'd liven up the time? You can go out in the rain, you know."

Jewel ignores me. She snorts, refuses to eat, keeps her backbone hair standing up. I finish milking, turn her loose and let her back out the door. The argument resumes.

Back in the house I put the milk in the refrigerator. Usually, I have a few people who want my extra milk. Now I'm filling the refrigerator and should make more cheese, except I'm still eating the last batch. Maybe I'll make some ricotta and use it in lasagna. Something to fill the time as the rain goes on and on. I'm sick of it.

I decide to take a leisurely shower and relax. Maybe I can watch a good mystery tonight. Or Justin brought home some westerns the last time he was here. I can heat a couple of frozen burritos for dinner. I need to start using up the food in the freezer just in case the electricity goes out.

After the movie, I turn on the outside light to watch the rain for a time. The drops shine as they fall to splash on the mud. At least the wind has died down. Maybe the storm will pass tomorrow.

It was a good day. My clothes are all clean and dry. So am I. Much of the house is clean. I turn off the light and go to bed shoving Sassy over so we both fit.

Day 6 The Briefcase

Rain still beats its drum on the roof when I wake up in the morning. My bedside battery clock ticks. Under this sound, the house seems quiet. "Let's get up, Sassy. It's time."

I pull on some clothes, totter my way to the bathroom and flip the switch. Nothing. Maybe the bulb burned out. I try the bedroom light. Nothing.

"Well, Sassy, the electricity is out. I guess we'll be eating a lot of frozen food before it ruins."

Back in the bathroom I turn off the shut off valve below the toilet. I will bring in a couple of buckets of rain water to pour in the tank to flush it. No electricity means no water pump leaving the house without water.

"You know, Sassy, as much as I want the rain to stop, we'll need the water." Out in the kitchen I look at the coffeemaker. No electricity, no coffeemaker. There is an old, really old, jar of instant in the cupboard.

I'd meant to get a new stove. My present one was inherited from Mrs. Watson and is of unknown age. The one really good thing about it now is that I can light the burners with a match. New stoves won't let you do that. One reason to have a propane stove out here. You can't light an electric stove and I hate cold canned food. I get a pan of water, light a front burner and put the water on to heat. I do love my coffee in the morning.

No electricity means no radio. No weather reports. No news. My world is now this place and only this place.

Walking out to the barn, I check the bucket. Another nine inches overnight. I switch it for an empty one so I can take the water to the bathroom. The continuous roar of running water surrounds me. When I set the pail and tote down, it hits me. "No electricity, no refrigerator. What am I going to do with the milk?"

The heavy clouds do keep air temperatures down in the seventies, but the milk will spoil in a day or two, maybe less. I could make cheese, but I still have some to eat and it will spoil fast when the refrigerator starts warming up. Reluctantly I decide to dump this morning's milk.

Squawking greets me in the hen house. The chickens are indignant, or seem so. They crowd their door awking at me. Before having the chickens, I hadn't realized how many sounds they make. This one is definitely an unhappy one.

"Sorry. The door stays closed until the rain stops. Don't gripe to me. Gripe at the rain." I dump feed in the feeder to distract them. The rain gutter fills the water fount so they have water for the day.

The goats are up and grouchy when I take the first round of hay out. Precious sideswipes Hope. She runs to the far end of the hay trough leaving Precious hogging a quarter of the trough while four goats crowd in on the lower third. Priscilla is in between enjoying her status conferred by her friendship with Precious.

That was another surprise about the goats. They form friendships and are very loyal to their friends. The pair will eat together, sleep together, defend and follow each other in the pasture.

After milking Precious, I peek out the door before letting her back out into the barn. The four have spread out around Priscilla and are eating at top speed. As soon as I let Precious out, the four race back to the far end again.

When milking is done, I put out more hay. I carry the tote out around the barn lot and dump it into the ravine. This has moved another couple of feet further up until it is almost full. The tree is no longer leaning over the ravine, it is down crushing part of the barn lot fence.

It will take a chainsaw to cut the tree up. Justin has one, a big one with a twenty-inch bar on it. I can pick the monster up, but there is no way I am going to use it. When that chain is racing around the bar, it will cut whatever it gets close to including legs. The monster is too big and heavy for me to handle safely.

And Justin won't be coming back. He won't help clear up this tangled mess. He'll want to leave it for whoever buys the place, if he can make me sell, if he can find anyone willing to buy the place. "And selling is beginning to look like my only option." My shoulders slump, defeat sneaking into my thoughts. "How can I take care of the place by myself? I can't. I don't have the money. I'm not big enough, not strong enough. I don't know about engines." Tears sting my eyes.

A bellow makes me jump. Is one of the steers in trouble? I haven't been over to check on them since the rain started. And I'm not eager to cross that bridge now water is racing by only a foot or so below it.

Another bellow is definitely coming from down toward the driveway. And there is an answering call from down the road. What are my steers doing out on the road? Why would they go out into that river?

I set the tote down and run toward the driveway. I need to close the gate as I don't need them up in the yard. They need to go back to the hill pasture.

A calf is walking up the driveway. It's young, maybe a couple of months old. Its mother must be coming up the road. "Shoo! Turn around!" I put my umbrella down feeling the rain soak my hair and start down my back under the slicker as I shove the calf back down the driveway.

The gate hasn't been closed in years and is mired in grass and mud. The flood waters have washed much of this away or loosened it. "Come on, gate. Get out of the grass. Hurry up, before the rest of the cows get here." The gate pulls free and swings across the driveway.

"How do I get you down to the hill pasture drive? Lead rope? Range cubes for your mother? No, they'll get soaked and fall apart. Lead rope." I run back to the barn to grab a rope snagging the tote on the way by to leave in the milkroom.

Back at the driveway I slip around the gate and fasten it. Eight cows and a second calf are coming up through water to their knees. I hate wet feet. My boots aren't tall enough. I sigh and move into the water flowing down the road.

"Whoa!" The water grabs at me almost pulling me over and down the road. This will be a job. I edge out into the flow and down the road. I can feel the top of the culvert under my boots as I cross it. Another twenty feet takes me to the drive into the hill pasture. I climb out of the road river, kneel down to dump water out of my boots and slog up to open that gate.

Back down at the edge of the water I hesitate. Before I was moving with the current. Now I will be going upstream. But the cows are crowding up into the driveway, not coming on down the road.

The current is swift and pushes against me as I struggle back across the culvert and up to the drive. Moving up through the cows, I stand by the gate. Umbrellas are scary to the goats. Maybe I can spook the cows. I get the umbrella bringing it out the gate. I open and close the umbrella several times. The cows move down the driveway, but not into the flooded road.

"So much for that idea. What next?" I toss the umbrella over the gate into the yard. Moving down the driveway I put the lead rope around the calf's neck. "Maybe your mama will follow you. Let's go, little one."

The calf does not want to go into the water again. I insist. We are a rough match weight wise. The calf has four feet, all planted in reverse. I move to one side, then the other to throw the calf off balance. And we are off on the trip down the road, the calf bellowing frantically. Answering bellows come from the cow. And she starts to follow. The others follow her.

With the current to help, the small herd arrives at the hill pasture drive and climbs back up out of the water. I slip the lead rope off the calf. The cows move up the drive toward the pasture except for one. She stands on the slope going up to the hill pasture staring down the road.

"Your calf went up the drive. Shoo." A faint cry comes from down the road. The cow bellows blowing my ear drums out. "Where is your calf?" Another bellow reverberates in my head. A faint answer seeps through the echo and I stare down the road.

There's movement down the road another fifty feet or so. A calf is struggling to stay standing as the current pushes it against a tree. "I see it." I hook the lead rope to a belt loop, wrap it around my waist, move back into the water and down toward the calf.

Swirling water shoves me down the road now sloping gently down. It rolls up my legs breaking into muddy eddies going around them. It pulls loose gravel out from under my boots.

Forty feet of road and I turn to cross the road to the calf. Water surges around my legs trying to push me further down the road. And the road drops out beneath my feet. The ditch!

I'm on my side flying by the calf and down the road. The water tries to billow up over my head. I spit mud out struggling to keep my head above the voracious flood carrying me down. My feet try to brace against the gravel bottom. It crumbles and slides out from under them. There's nothing to grab. I open my mouth to breathe and get a mouthful of muddy water.

A branch smashes into me. I grab it holding on with white knuckles and cramping hands and spitting out mud, retching to empty my stomach of water. I take a few shaky breaths. Forcing one hand to open I move it up the branch realizing I'm being smashed into a fallen tree. Hand over hand I pull myself upright and over toward where a fence is supposed to be, except it isn't there. The road berm is.

Standing on the berm, water racing around my legs pushing me toward the tree, I see I am at the end of the cow pasture, a quarter of a mile from home. This is one of the trees past the end of the pasture, one once lining the wet weather creek marking the end of the pasture and the property, now fallen across the road.

I can't stay here. I need to, must get back up the road. Shoving one leg forward, then the other, I move up the road berm. At each of the trees lining the road, I stop to rest.

My hands shake. My body shakes. Not with cold. Terror still grips me, turns my insides cold.

"Idiot! What a stupid fool I am. Justin told me to get out. The animals needed me. I needed him. And where is he? Not here! Imbecile! I know about the ditch. What's wrong with you, brain? Keep walking. Keep moving the feet. Sell? You bet I will. Staying here alone is lunacy."

And I'm back to the calf. It must be cold and frightened too. I turn it to face up the road and force it up the road berm. It resists. The water resists. The distance to the cow pasture gate diminishes inches at a time.

The cow pasture drive offers a way to cross that deadly ditch. I use the lead rope to drag the calf out onto the road. The cow is out on the road in front of the hill pasture drive bellowing. The calf is answering. It's only another ten feet.

The calf is now trying to pull me along and get to its mother. We are fighting the full current in water up to the calf's belly. I shove to keep the calf from being washed away. And then the calf is by its mother's side, reaching under for the teat and a drink of reassurance I could use too. The cow goes back up the drive followed by her calf and me fumbling to take the lead rope off the calf. They go up into the pasture.

I stand staring up the flooded road. The driveway is thirty feet away. I have to reach it. I can't make my feet go back into the water. I'm trembling. My legs want to collapse under me. Rain pours down on my head and runs down my body. It's cold. I need to get back to the house.

I walk back down to the end of the drive. Can I make it up another thirty feet? I don't know. I have to.

The bridge. Maybe I can cross it instead.

Something is coming down the road. I watch. It's another calf. I grab a leg as it washes by and pull. It's heavy and I can only get the front part up on the drive out of the water. It lays flat on the ground, limp. I shake it, try to dump water out of its mouth, pound on its side.

"Breathe!" I pound on the calf's side. I shake its head. "Come on, breathe!

The eyes are glazed. The tongue hangs out of its mouth. It's dead. I sit down. The current gradually pulls the calf back into the current. It speeds away leaving me wondering how many others are being carried away. Shuddering I realize how close I came to joining it.

Where are these cows coming from? They must be from the fields further up the valley. They had no place to go until the flood washed out the fences. No one came to rescue them before the rain started. I hope the others made it up onto the hills.

The body is far down the road now, about where I was when the current grabbed me. That water is so strong. I can feel its pull, its grasp not wanting to let me go. The rain runs down my back, down my face washing tears out of my eyes.

Pushing down on the ground, I stand up, take a step back into the water to push my way up toward the driveway and the house. Feeling the pull of the water, how it drags the dirt out from under my feet, pushing me, dragging me, trying to take me away to join that calf, fear tightens my muscles and clutches my chest.

I back out of the water and stare down the road. Nothing seems to be moving down the road. Maybe no more cows made it this far. Maybe they got up onto the hills. I hope so.

"I have to go back to the house. It's too cold and wet to stay here. I can do this. Step into that water. It's only thirty feet." Except I can't make my feet move. I turn to follow the drive up the slope into the hill pasture crossing over to the gate toward the ravine. Opening the gate, I slip through and close it again. The bridge is wet, but still above the flood raging below it. It's five feet wide, wide enough for the tractor to cross. It's strong enough to hold the tractor. I inch across staying in the center trying not to listen to or see the water pouring down the ravine just below the wooden planks. Trying not to think what would happen if I slipped off the bridge.

Opening and closing the barn lot gate, I walk up to the barn. Inside, the goats stare at me. I find I am crying and shaking. I should be dead, drowned like that calf. If it weren't for the fallen tree, I would be. I am an idiot to be out here alone. Justin, I need you.

The goats aren't out of hay, but close. Mindlessly, shaking uncontrollably, I put out more before going across to the house with the rain washing the last of the muddy water off my clothes which I shed in the mud porch along with the boots turning them upside down to drain.

My body is coated with mud. I step back out into the rain and let it wash off. Inside I find a towel to dry off, wrap myself in a bathrobe, find Sassy, sit down in my recliner hugging her and crying.

When I sit up to dry my eyes, I decide to start cleaning the bedroom. It's pretty clean in there already, but I need something to do. I walk in and look out the window which faces the lower part of the yard.

"Another cow. I guess I better go send it down to the hill pasture." I reach for some clothes. "No electricity. No washer. No dryer. I'll put the wet stuff on again to do this."

Out on the porch I pick up my wet jeans. They're cold as well as wet. Gritting my teeth, I pull them on feeling bits of sand scrape my legs. The shirt is hard to put on as the sleeves cling shut. I just can't put the wet socks on again and shove my feet into the wet boots without them.

No umbrella. It's down by the gate. I walk out feeling the rain sluice through my hair and down my back. Maybe it will wash some of the dirt out of my clothes.

Four cows with calves are crowding up against the gate. I pick up my umbrella and flick it open. The cow next to the gate spooks shoving the others down the driveway as she flees from this monster.

I open the gate wide enough to let myself out with the now furled umbrella. After closing the gate, I flick the umbrella open again. This group moves back down to the edge of the road.

"Get on down the road! Move it!" I wave the umbrella, open and close it again. The cows with their calves wade back into the flood waters and move down the road. It seems strange to not hear them bawling. Their heads hang almost to the water as though they have given up all hope. They trudge through the current crossing the culvert. One drops into a hole on the other side, but swims to where it has footing again.

Another twenty feet and the group clambers out onto the drive up to the hill pasture. I watch them walk up the slope and disappear toward the gate I left open. There are now a dozen cows, my eight steers and seven calves hiding up in the woods as the rain continues.

I go back through the gate leaving it closed behind me and trudge back to the barn. The goats shouldn't need more hay, but I check. I see fresh hay on the barn floor and a partially empty hay trough.

"You better be eating this stuff." The goats stare at me dripping my way around with the hay. Their basin is half empty, so I pour a bucket of rain water in. In fact, I set the bucket where runoff from the roof will keep it filled. The goats will have plenty of water as long as the rain keeps coming down.

Back at the house, I shed my wet, dirty clothes again, dump the water out of my boots, turning them upside down to finish draining, then walk back out barefooted on the cement walk feeling the cool rain wash the dirt off of my body. I'm cold and a hot shower would help, but one is not available. I go into my house to towel off.

Dressed in bathrobe and slippers, I attack the bedroom. "What am I doing? This is beyond stupid. I don't want this. I want a nice little country place, big enough for my goats, chickens, children and me. Someplace that doesn't flood. Justin's right, we need to sell this place, find another one."

The only thing out of place is Justin's briefcase. "That was sloppy of him. I wonder if he's missed it yet. I wonder if the bank statement is in it. I would like to know how much money is in the account." I take it out to the kitchen table.

My stomach reminds me I skipped lunch. I open the refrigerator to get out fixings for a sandwich and find everything feels cool, not cold. The race to eat the contents before they spoil has started. I'm generous with the lunchmeat in my sandwich.

Sassy moves into my lap as soon as I sit down. I stare at the briefcase. "Justin's right. We need to sell this place to some other chump. All I need is five acres near a paved road. I want the illusion of country living, not the reality. I've had it up to here with the reality."

Memory of my wild ride down the ditch makes me shudder. "You almost lost me this morning, Sassy. Justin was right. I shouldn't be down here alone. We need to move to a smaller place, a safer place."

This place will be hard to sell, isolated as it is and the fences wiped out, the fallen trees. Buying a new place will take money. How much money is left in the account? The answer should be in that briefcase. I stare at it.

The briefcase belongs to Justin. I can hear my father telling me to never touch what belongs to someone else without their permission. I can't ask for permission. Besides, I'm sure he would say no.

But I'm Justin's wife. Those statements are for our joint account. I have a right to see them. I need to see them.

The briefcase isn't locked. It isn't mine. "You do not ever touch someone else's things without asking and getting permission," my father told me and grounded me for three days for wearing my sister's necklace without asking. "There are no exceptions. You do not do this."

I take the briefcase back into the bedroom returning it to the closet. There's time before evening chores. I'll do them early so I'm in before dark. I sit down in my recliner and open my book. Sassy joins me.

After the first paragraph, I lean back. "Those statements will be addressed to me too. Just because he handles our finances, doesn't mean I can't know about them. It may be his briefcase, but the contents belong to me too. I need to see those statements."

The briefcase belongs to Justin.

I look down at my book. It's another thriller, my favorite genre. The author is one of my favorites. Within three pages I'm lost, have no idea what I just read. "Sassy, I'm going to open that briefcase. After milking, I'm going to open that briefcase." This time I manage to read a couple of chapters, although they barely register, before milking time.

I check out the bedroom window. No more cows seem to be at the driveway gate so I put on clean, dry clothes. The socks soak through from the wet boots, but the rest of me feels better.

There are another eight inches in the bucket. "That makes forty-eight inches so far, a whole year's worth of rain in three days." I stare over to see the ravines are full and edging into the yard. "If this doesn't quit soon, the hill will flood. Then, what do we do? We have no place to go." Water laps at the bottom of the bridge, foaming up onto the planks. If these wash away, we can't get over on the hills.

The goats are ready for more hay. As I fill the hay trough, I tell the goats I'm going to find out how much money we have. It's important to them so they can keep eating, so they still have a home. I reassure each goat as I milk her that I will do everything I can to see we have a home. The answers are in the briefcase and I am going to find them.

Back in the house I get some frozen burritos out, except they aren't so frozen now. The refrigerator freezer is starting to thaw. Usually, I microwave them. Tonight, I heat them up in a frying pan and eat them slightly charred.

By now the house is getting dark. I light a few candles, one in each room. These are placed away from anything flammable. This old house would burn fast and I'm not eager to live in the barn with the goats.

I retrieve the briefcase from the closet, march out to the kitchen, set it on the table and open it. There is a divider over the bottom section and four folder pockets on the top along with a zippered pouch. I light a second candle setting both on the table so I can see better.

"Where should I start? Where would the account statements be? One of the folders."

A thick wad of papers is in the first folder. I place them in front of me and stare. "What's this? Stocks and bonds? We don't have any, do we? Justin does." I stare at the value of almost four hundred ninety thousand dollars. "This can't be ours."

Searching over the papers I find the account is in Justin's name only. It does seem to go back to before we were married. Maybe that's why I'm not on it.

"He could have told me about it. He's putting three thousand five hundred a month in it. How much is he making a month?"

I know long haul drivers make decent money, around four thousand a month. If he's putting that much in this account, he's not putting much in our joint account. He can't be putting in the six hundred I use every month. Where is that coming from?

This stack of papers goes back into its folder. The next stack comes out. "A savings account. Wait, this isn't our joint account. This is a St. Louis bank, not the local one. It's his account with five thousand in it. And I'm not on this one either."

When we got married, I closed out my personal accounts to move the money into a joint account to let Justin manage our finances. That's what wives were supposed to do. Justin put money in it too. Marriages had joint accounts.

Why didn't Justin? And why didn't he tell me about these accounts? And why is there so much money in these accounts? Why is he always saying we don't have enough money?

"How much does he put in this one? Deposits. A hundred dollars last month. Unless he's making a lot more than I think he is, he's not paying my bills."

These statements get put back. Two folders to go. I take out the next stack. "At last. The local bank. Here's the savings account and checking account."

I look at the first one, then check all of the others for this year. There are no deposits, only withdrawals. Six hundred a month. The checking account shows deposits matching the withdrawals.

"He lied to me. He's been lying to me. I'm not using his money. This is my money, what I had left after paying for this place. Did he even put any money in to buy it?"

I'm sure Justin won't contribute a penny for a new place if he didn't contribute to buy this one. Unless I can sell the place for enough to buy somewhere else, I'm stuck here. "Well, there's a little under twenty thousand left in the account. Since I take out six hundred a month, I'm good for a couple of years. I won't be buying anything extra like fencing, lumber or steers. And they will have to pay their way from now on. I need a job."

I put the statements back in the pocket and take the papers out of the fourth one. These are our birth certificates, driving certifications, vehicle titles, powers of attorney, deed for the property and our marriage license. I put them back.

"What's in here?" I pull the zipper to find Justin's pay stubs for this year. "Like I thought, about four thousand a month. The liar. He's not giving me a penny."

The pay stubs go back in the pouch. I sit back staring at the wall. Justin has been lying to me. He told me he was putting money into our account. He wasn't and isn't. Had he put any in after opening the account? I don't know. I do know where his money has been going: the other bank account and the investment account. The ones without my name on them.

Justin complained he worked and I took his money. His money was going to fix up the place. He was lying.

Under the divider is a stack of folders. It's late. I don't want any more ugly surprises. The candles are half burned. I'll look through them in the morning. I close the briefcase, blow out the candles and go to bed listening to the rain beating on the roof.

"If Justin didn't put any money in for buying this place, it should be mine, not ours. It's been my money, not his, paying for repairs, equipment, everything." I stare up toward the ceiling hidden in darkness, letting these revelations sink in. I've never owned anything on my own before. Except his name is on the deed. And I doubt he will take it off. After all, I am his wife and everything I have is supposed to be his. But I don't like it. He lied to me.

Day 7 Enough Rain

My eyes snap open to the same grey light out the window, the same drumming on the roof. I pull the sheet over my head squeezing my eyes shut wanting to hide for the day. When will this rain end? This is day four of this stupid weather. Water was over the top of the ravines last night. The yard could be flooded. If it isn't, it will be by tonight.

Sighing I flip the sheet off. One thing about owning livestock: you can't hide in bed all day feeling sorry for yourself. They are hungry. They depend on you to get up and out to the barn.

Sassy stretches and curls up again. She can sleep in. "Lazy. When are you getting up? When I rattle your dish?"

The briefcase is still on the kitchen table. "He lied to me. I'll find out more after chores." I put water on the stove to heat and scrape instant coffee into my mug. There's enough to last another day or two.

My mother used to talk about perking coffee. And expresso pours hot water through ground coffee. I have plenty of coffee for the coffeemaker and that pours hot water over the grounds. "I should have a strainer around here somewhere. I saw it when I cleaned up the kitchen. Where is it? That drawer!"

The water's hot. I stir some into the instant. After gathering my equipment and drinking a mug of coffee, I'm awake.

On the mud porch I stare at my wet boots. Even after draining all night, I know the insides are soggy and cold. I grit my teeth, shove my feet into them and shiver. "Where's the sun? This is August, hot, sunny August. Rain, rain, go away. Come again some other day. Like in a month or two."

My umbrella tries to open. Wind is shoving back against it. I jerk it and it locks open. Rain is slanting under it to soak my legs where my rain slicker has blown open. The trees are making a roaring sound as I struggle over to the barn trying to angle and hang onto the umbrella.

Inside the milk room door, I stand and look out. The trees across the ravine behind the chicken yard are more than swaying. They dip like grass blown in the wind. There's a sharp snap as a branch drops to the ground.

The roofing tin is rattling. It's screwed down tight and shouldn't blow off. It better not blow off.

The goats have their backbone fur standing up and tails raised. They snort at me as I put out fresh hay. No one comes over.

"It's only the wind. Come on over and eat." I scratch behind ears and sides of necks. The goats crowd around me. "You're safe in here." I grab a handful of hay and hold it under a couple of noses. Precious grabs it. "Look out for the fingers!" She now starts eating hay. The others join her.

I walk to the door to check out the ravine. The water level has dropped below the bridge. I'll have to check the bucket.

The goats still crowd the far end of the barn. I bring them in one at a time to eat grain and get milked. They stand shivering, refusing to eat more than a mouthful or two. They crowd the door and me eager to get out to join the others.

Getting a bucket of feed, I cautiously open my umbrella angling it into the wind and start toward the chicken house. The wind pushes the umbrella down. The wind shifts jerking it upward until I get it angled into the wind only to have the wind shift so I have to move it again.

A sliding, swishing sound stops me. "What is that? Where is it coming from?" I swivel around staring off around the yard and across to the hills. Beyond the end of the yard a huge oak is falling. It swishes through the trees in its downward path. I hear some snap off and a thud as the oak hits the ground.

The upper branches extend across the ravine onto the rocks at the end of the yard. "I need a chainsaw. I'll have to find the money to buy one. I wonder if I can sell or trade that big one of Justin's. I bought it. I guess I can sell it. He's not going to use it."

At the chicken house, even a full feeder isn't enough to cheer the flock up much. A few stand in the doorway looking out. "Back in here, chickens. It's still raining. You're still stuck in the house."

I grab the water fount. The chickens had tossed dirt and feed up into it scratching around on the floor. The water from the downspout washes it off and out. I fill it with fresh water and set it back in the house. That endless water supply is the one thing I will miss once the rain stops.

On the way back to the barn I hear another tree fall. I haven't opened the umbrella as the wind is too fierce so rain blows in my face. The slicker hood blows off my head and water runs down my neck.

On the way to the house, I check the bucket. Only five inches is in it. "The rain slowed down, but the wind picked up. Both ways, I lose."

Standing in the kitchen, I start to put water on for oatmeal. "Oatmeal won't spoil. I better eat some of that food up." Breakfast is a sandwich of deli meat. Maybe I'll fry up the rest of it with a couple of eggs for dinner tonight. The frozen broccoli is thawing so I can have that with the meat and eggs.

Munching on my sandwich, I stand staring out the window. The drops seem smaller. The drumming is softer. And the sky seems lighter.

After eating, I go back to stare at the briefcase. Before I opened it, I trusted Justin. I didn't agree with him, but I trusted him. Part of me wants to go back to that time. I love my husband. There must be an explanation. If only I could call him. The phone is still dead.

I sit down and open the briefcase. This time I take out the pile of folders under the divider. Each one has a year on the tab. I take out the one for last year.

Income tax forms are in the folder along with all the various other forms needed. I find Justin has done our taxes separately. Mine has the joint account on it, nothing else. His has his bank interest, investment returns, income. Maybe this is why he doesn't put anything in the joint account. It would mess up the income tax stuff.

I've never done income tax forms. My father had me as a dependent until I got married. Then Justin did the taxes. All I did was sign where he told me to sign.

I put the papers back in the folder and close it. The other folders have tax forms for the years on the tabs. Looking over them, the only thing I can really see is how Justin's accounts have grown over the years. And mine has just as steadily shrunk. Why didn't he have me invest some of my money?

Justin never talked to me about money or finances. My father never did either. My mother taught me about budgets as my father gave her so much money to last the month and she had to make it stretch. I'm good at that. I don't know anything else.

"Mindy, girl, you better learn something. That money will run out and you will be in trouble." I get up to stare out the window. "I'll need money coming in. Even if I don't stay here, I'll want someplace to live unless I go back to driving. No, that's not an option. I'm done driving."

That puts me at odds with Justin. He wants me to drive as his team. We did make a good team. We had fun going places. The money was good.

Money. Why does he keep his a secret? Why does he lie to me about it? If we were really a team, he wouldn't.

What else can I do? I have no skills except what I learned on the place. And jobs are hard to come by in town, mostly minimum wage and part time. That won't pay the bills and won't give me time for the place.

Justin is right. The place will never pay its way. The steers pay for themselves and a little over. I can't have many more than the eight and have enough pasture. The hay brings in a little, if I have it and won't this year. If the hay in the cow barn is okay, I could hold the steers over and sell them as beef next year. But then I'll need money to buy calves in the spring.

I could sell this place. I love it, the isolation, the hills, the peace. And being stranded? No electricity? Every big storm leaves me both. And being alone here is stupid. But, could I sell the place? Who else would move into this out-of-the-way place? And, unless I sell it, I can't move.

Why does he insist the place pay for itself? Pay its way? Homes don't pay their way, they're where you live.

Money. It's all about money. I don't have enough. I don't know how to get more. And Justin has locked his away, his secret fortune. Why? Is he afraid I will spend it?

My eyes blink away moisture and focus out the window. "The rain is stopping! Sassy, the rain is stopping. It's finally over." I walk out onto the mud porch to stare out across the yard. The grey has lightened to almost having a little sun. The rain still falls, but only small drops, more mist than rain.

"Wonderful! The road crew will clear the road in a week or so, maybe sooner. The electricity and phone will be back on. I can get to town. I can go to the bank and talk to someone about the account. I can call Justin and ask him about the money." I pull on my boots to go outside.

When I step into the yard, even the mist has stopped. Finally stopped. Overhead, light grey clouds are broken. Blue sky peeks out between them as they race off taking the wind and rain with them to plague people northeast of me.

A patch of warm sunlight surrounds me. I spin around laughing. My face begins to ache from the grin plastered on it.

Wind rushes through the treetops. They sway, but not like before. Checking the bucket, I find a final ten inches, five more than this morning when I didn't dump the bucket. I've gotten fifty-eight inches of rain in four days.

At the barn the downspout still has a thin stream flowing. "I better fill the goat's trough now, while the barrel can refill. Should have done it this morning." The water supply has ended. Now there are the containers in the house and the barrels. When those are gone, only muddy water is left.

The water basin holds a bucket's worth of water giving room for this last to not run off. The goats need a week's worth, enough to last until the electricity is back on.

The goats are peeking out the barn door looking at the fallen tree. Precious takes a step out. Priscilla tries one too. The other four push them out and a mad dash ensues. They stand among and on the branches tearing off leaves as though they are starving to death.

I get the egg bucket on my way over to the chicken house. The hens pile out on top of each other getting out of their door. I walk into the almost empty house to gather eggs early. Their yard is mud. That mud will track in on the eggs and I hate cleaning off dirty, muddy eggs. Besides, it takes water.

After leaving the eggs on the kitchen counter, I walk around the edge of the yard. Water levels are dropping in the ravines. Trees are down. The big oak at the back of the yard. One behind the orchard fence. One in front of the chicken yard. The one in the barn lot now being devoured. Another is leaning out over the ravine and will fall behind the barn. Maybe someone will come and cut them up for firewood so I don't have to.

Walking down the driveway I find only a shallow creek over the main road. Deep ditches are cut on each side of the culvert. Walking along the road isn't dangerous now unless I count dropping into the potholes as a problem. I can see the big trees down across the road at the end of the cow pasture and the far end of the hay field. Both fields still have standing water across much of their expanses.

All the gates and gate posts as well as the corner posts with their braces and the braces in the long stretches seem to be standing. The fence posts I see along the road are leaning toward the field. The wire is covered with debris. I need to move the steers back into their field as the hill pasture doesn't have enough grass for them and the extra cows. That means standing the posts and wire back up or driving new posts I don't have and putting the wire on them.

I stare down the fence line. There is a post every ten feet. The cow pasture is almost a quarter mile long and half that wide. That's about four hundred posts. I remember putting all of them up. Justin and I traded off driving them in with the post driver. It took us a week to put the posts in and another two weeks to get the wire up around just the cow pasture.

Justin's not here. Justin's not coming here. I'm alone. No one will help do this. "This is insane. No way can I keep the fences, let alone the place up by myself. No, I have to sell and find a smaller place."

And, if I can't sell the place? What then? What about now?

Now I will enjoy the sunshine. After close to four days of rain, almost sixty inches of rain, the hot summer sun feels fantastic. My muscles relax and seem to stretch. My damp clothes are drying and itching a bit.

Birds are calling. A red-tailed hawk screeches overhead. Deer are coming out into the cow pasture to graze except the grass is plastered to the ground and muddy where it's not covered with water.

I walk over the bridge up into the hill pasture. My steers and the other cows are out grazing. Calves are lying flat soaking up heat. From up here I can look far up and down the valley. Steam rises from the trees and pastures. My troubles evaporate in the warmth. I can do this. I can.

Anything seems possible all evening. Milking and chores go fast. That night the sunset has scattered deep salmon pink clouds. I stand at the window to watch. "Sassy, if you could see color, you'd see a glorious sight. Pink is a promise of a warm day ahead."

Even being inside with only the candles for light isn't depressing. Staying inside is impossible. I stand outside in the yard staring up "Look at all the stars. Hello, stars. It's great to see you again." A bat flutters erratically chasing moths across the sky over my head. The air is warm and moist.

Over my dinner of fried deli meat with eggs and soggy broccoli, I start a list of things to do for cleaning up the place. I better start with the freezers. In fact, I can do that now.

There isn't much I can do about the chopped peppers or meat or frozen burritos and such. I take out the tomato sauce now partially thawed and dump it into a stock pot to boil. I have jars and lids to can it and put on some water to heat to warm the jars.

While the tomato sauce heats, I go back to my list. After taking a look around, I put down in capital letters to fix the cow pasture fence. "I have to move those steers and cows across the road soon. Then the goats can move back into the hill pasture. I guess the goats can eat the downed trees until then."

The tomato sauce is boiling. It's so acid I can hot pack it. I warm the jars, pour the hot water out of one, fill it with hot tomato sauce. Screwing the lid down tight, I hastily toss the hand towel on the counter to set the filled jar down. Soon a dozen jars sit cooling on the towel. The first one pings as the lid pulls down to secure the seal. The others follow suit.

"So much for that. I wish I could do more stuff. There's no way I can eat it all before it spoils."

I look over at the list of two items. "There's so much more. Cleaning up the fallen trees. What do I do with the branches? And there's a lot more fencing to repair."

Grabbing up Sassy, I hug her. "Oh, Sassy, I'm doomed. I can't do it. Everywhere I looked this afternoon, there were messes to clean up. What can I do? I'm only one person. Justin, I hate you." Sassy struggles to get down out of my falling tears. My head sinks onto my arms on the table as she slides free.

Later I blow out the candles and crawl into bed snuggling down under a sheet. Sassy curls up against me.

It's dark. Dim light from the stars and crescent moon show outside the window. Inside no light shines. The clocks are dark.

It's quiet. No rain on the roof. No refrigerator or freezer hum. Only the quiet vibrating with faint purrs as Sassy falls asleep and the turmoil in my head keep me company for a time.

Part Three

Facing Reality

Day 8 Flood Waters Recede

A dim grey hint of sunrise lights my window in the morning when I open my eyes. Birds are calling outside. Sassy's warmth against my stomach and the house's quiet lull me back to sleep.

I'm getting ready to go to town. Library books are due. The phone needs reporting. Do I need groceries? Feed? I'll get my mail, read the local paper, drop by the bank.

The bank. Justin lied to me about the bank. I'm awake.

One look out the window reminds me I won't be driving to town today or tomorrow. "I guess I'll be trimming branches and fixing fence today. There are only four hundred posts to do." My shoulders slump.

The few puffy clouds I can see through the window are turning white. I slide out of bed leaving Sassy curled up. She stretches out, yawns and goes back to sleep.

The last of the instant coffee gets scraped into my mug. "So much for this sorry excuse for coffee. I'll try expresso tomorrow." Grabbing the milk pail and tote, pulling on my boots, I head for the barn.

Instead of water on the yard, there is mud. It cakes under and on my boots. By the time I get to the barn, I'm lifting weights moving my feet. Some of it shakes off at the door. Most of it tracks into the milk room.

There are no goats in the barn when I fill the hay trough. Looking out the door I see them standing on tree branches eating leaves. Most of what they can reach is gone. After chores, I'll try to cut some of the branches sticking up out of reach.

"Precious!" Nothing. "Priscilla!" Nothing. "Maybe the chickens will be happy to see me."

Chickens jam the door on their way outside. Their yard is gooey mud that soon encases all their feet. Muddy eggs tonight.

The water fount trough is filled with feed, nest hay and dirt. There's just enough water left inside to wash the stuff out. The now empty feed bucket conveys water from the rain barrel to the fount. Once it's set back in the yard, the chickens are set for the morning.

I open the milk room door and call for the goats to come in. Nothing. "Precious! Get in here. Precious." Another call from the barn door gets her to look my direction. She starts to take another mouthful of leaves, stops, drops down from the branch to race for the barn. The other goats join vying to be first in the open door. I beat them only because I'm already in the barn and close the door before the whole herd is in arguing over the milk stands.

Pairs of goats can again come in as their gobbling days are over. Most of the milk goes into the ravine again. I miss my refrigerator.

Breakfast is more like dinner as I cook up more thawing food. Charbroiled burritos may be edible, but are not my choice. Still, it's that or throw them out. And some of the food must be thrown out now, mostly chopped peppers turned to mush and my cheese now soured. Maybe I will bring the milk in tonight and make more cheese.

"Sassy, you'll like dinner and lunch. Hamburger. How many ways can I fix it? Too bad I don't have any bread left. I suppose I could make pancakes for bread."

My cat ignores me. She's looking out the windows watching birds hopping around the yard. I join her. They seem happy to have sunny weather again.

"There's no hope the road crew will get here today. Sassy, we're stuck. I can't cut up those fallen trees. Even if I could, the road is a mess. Well, I need to clean up here and go look over the cow pasture and hay field. Those fences won't fix themselves."

Wishing Justin were here, someone to talk to, someone to help, I pull on my muddy boots and walk to the cow pasture. There is a short stretch of wire between the first corner and the gate post. The metal posts are leaning toward the field.

I open the gate leaving it swung into the pasture. At the post I stoop a bit to get leverage and push upward. It shifts. The weight is enormous. Leaves, branches, twigs and mud are piled on the woven wire and will have to come off before

I can move the post. And I will need some way to pull on the posts as I cannot do more than a couple this way, maybe.

"This is a tractor job. Except the ground is so soft and muddy. And the road has those ditches. I think I'll walk around and look things over."

Walking down the fence line I remember putting it up. Justin insisted on stringing a line so the fence would be straight. Every post was ten feet from its neighboring posts. The gate, bracing and corner posts, all railroad ties, were sunk two feet deep with cross braces and wire braces. Every inch of that two feet was an argument with rocks. Justin taught me a lot of new cuss words.

"All that work paid off now. All the gate posts, brace posts and corner posts are still up." I turn the corner and start off across the pasture. These metal posts are like the others, pushed toward the pasture and covered with debris. A couple of big branches lie across the wire. "My bow saw will handle these."

Even the corner posts back by the creek are still standing and solid. There are some trees down in the creek bed. Only one fell over the fence and that's only the top branches. "More bow saw work."

In the center of the pasture fence Justin dug out an oxbow so creek water flowed into the pasture to water the steers. It's clogged with gravel and will need digging out again. He used a scoop now sitting up in the implement line. Except I can't change the implements easily except for the fork and the special bush hog designed for easy attachment.

"Guess I'll be digging this out by hand. And the creek's further away. Maybe I'll try to attach that scoop. It isn't that big."

The last stretch across the pasture is like the other end. The posts lean toward the field. They need to be pushed out as the tractor can't work around the trees in the wet weather creek section. "Wonder where that come-along is. It should be hanging against the tractor shed wall."

Back on the road, I walk down to the hay field. The grass lies flat on the ground. It will not stand up again. "No hay from this field." I clamber over the fence also leaning into the field rather than walk down to the gate which is still standing with a small pond under it. "Too wet for the tractor here."

This fence across the field is like the other side. The posts lean into the field. The far side is like the cow pasture too except more limbs are on the fence.

As I approach the far end, vultures fly out of the trees. "I guess a cow didn't make it out of that pasture." This end fence leans into the hay field. I climb over and walk through the trees to the neighboring pasture and crawl through the barbed wire strands.

The stench of dead, rotting meat hangs in the air. I see a cow and a couple of calves smashed up against the trees. Looking up toward the road I see another cow. This one is standing up. Her tail swings up across her back.

"You're alive! Why are you standing there?" I walk up. Barbed wire is wrapped around the cow's legs. On her far side is a calf trying to nurse and pushing wire into her udder so the cow tries to kick.

"I'll need wire cutters and my fence tool. Be back soon." Going back into my hay field, I walk up the fence line a bit faster, through the gate leaving it open into the field and up to my workshop. Back down the road, over the fence and to the cow.

"You stand still. Move it, calf. These small bolt cutters will make short work of that barbed wire. Just stand still." The cow's front legs are free.

"Hold still. Quit that!" Muddy tail in the face is icky. I sidle up to the cow to keep from being kicked. Cows can kick sideways and it hurts. Three cuts and the wire peels off this leg. The cow backs up and tries to pull into the pasture.

"I need a rope. Why didn't I bring one? Stop, cow. I can't cut you loose, if you don't stop." I get around the cow to her other side. She pushes me back and forth as I try to position the bolt cutters. Time after time I get ready to cut only to have the wire jerked out of place. One wire done. Second wire done. Now she's pulling away, her leg stretched back with wire wrapped just above her hoof. I cut it just above the wrap. "Maybe it will fall off now." The cow is headed across the pasture, calf in tow, looking for her herd.

There is an answering call to the cow's bellow. Looking across the creek I can see cows on the other side of the flood. She paces along the creek as they talk back and forth. Finally, she stops and begins searching for grass to eat. There are muddy clumps here and there. "Guess you'll be coming down the road in a day or two. I better get that fence fixed."

Walking up to the fence, there is no fence. Even the corner post is knocked to the ground and covered with debris. It's firm enough to walk on so the cows will be out on the road once they get across the creek.

A big oak tree lies across the road ten feet further down the road. The trunk is a good two feet in diameter. "Forget the bowsaw. Maybe I can cut some of the branches for the goats. This is definitely a job for a big chainsaw. Have fun, road crew."

After lunch, I return to the cow pasture. There are two deep ditches on either side of the culvert. The road department would fill them with gravel I don't have and I need to drive the tractor down the road. I do have lots of debris to drag off the fence.

A few passes with a hoe convince me debris removal is a hands-on affair. One armload at a time I dump debris into the ditch closest to the fence. "This is too slow. I need bigger loads. I can't get the wheelbarrow across either. Maybe I can fill feed sacks."

Feed sacks are not at all cooperative. The tops close as soon as a piece of debris touches the edges. "There's got to be a way." I toss debris on a flat sack. Three armloads and I pull the edges together like a sling. Dump. Pile. Dump. I'm a robot in mindless movement.

Dump. Pile. Dump. Ten feet done. Twenty feet done. Thirty feet and I'm to the gate posts. And the first ditch is piled over the edges.

The next thirty feet, three posts worth, fills the other ditch. "Have to do more tomorrow. Time to do chores."

It's still light after chores. I go back to clear off some more fence. It's faster now because I'm dumping the debris onto the edge of the road. I can barely see walking back to the house with a stomach screaming about dinner.

"Hey, Sassy, more hamburger. It sure saves on cat food." The frozen veggies are gone, so I open a can of corn. "Maybe I should plant some greens, lettuce and stuff in the morning."

Out of habit, I check the phone. Still dead. The refrigerator light is still out, so the electricity is still off. Candlelight works, but I miss my lights. Tonight, it doesn't matter much as I'm too tired to read, almost too tired to pull off my dirty clothes before falling into bed.

Day 9 Learning to Fix Fence

My eyes open. Dawn is peeking in my window. I move a leg. Pain. Every movement brings painful protests from muscles I'd long forgotten about. They hadn't forgotten about me.

"Hot shower," I mumble inching my way to the bathroom. "I need a hot shower."

Except there is no hot shower as there is no electricity and no water. "Justin, I hate you. You said we don't need a generator. They fix the lines in a day or two. Yeah, right."

I use a little water to wash my face. That opens my eyes. By the time I struggle into the kitchen the aches are subsiding into dull throbs. A cup of weak expresso gets me moving out to a barn bereft of goats. They are finishing off the tree, but gladly mob the milk room for grain. All through milking my mind worries at what I should do about the place, about the lies. Today I keep the milk to make vinegar set cheese as it's easier and lasts longer than mozzarella.

The chickens race out into the sunshine. The mud in their yard is firming up as is the mud in the yard. It's still too soft for the tractor.

I cook up all of the hamburger that is left hoping it will last another day or two. Sassy is delighted with a bowlful. More food is ruined in the freezer. I'll dump it out before tackling the fence.

"I wonder how fast lettuce grows. I better get some planted this morning."

By mid-morning, the freezer is half emptied, cheese is cooling in the pot and rows of red and green leaf lettuce, radishes, mizuna and spinach are planted. I look at the post driver in the shed. Unless I take the wire off the posts, I'll have to use the sledge hammer. I grab it and head over to the cow pasture.

"The debris is off the wire. Heave ho. Stand up post." The ground is soft and the post pushes up. Three taps with the sledge and I'm on to the next one. Three posts and this section to the gate is standing up again, weaving drunkenly, but standing.

There's a long stretch of wire on the other side of the gate. The gate posts help standing up the first post, but then the others sag, even after tapping them in, pulled down by those beyond them. Doggedly I keep going down the row half a dozen posts.

"This isn't working. They look awful." I stomp back and do them again.

"Hey, those first two look okay."

The routine begins. Clear debris for three lengths of fence. Move down three posts. Push up a post and tap. Move back down the fence, push and tap. Move down the fence, push and tap. It takes four posts to get the first one standing up, but only if I turn the brain and its worries off.

The brain turns off as the afternoon leaves me moving like a robot clearing, pushing and tapping. By chore time I'm half way to the brace posts. After chores, I just clear debris getting a head start for tomorrow. Eight lengths of fence leave me close to groping my way back to the house.

"Microwave, oh, microwave, how I miss you. Zap, zap and dinner is hot." Instead, I heat hamburger on the stove, side it with fried potato and canned peas.

Tonight, I stay awake through ten pages of my thriller. Heading to bed I find my muscles are stiffening. I snuggle under a blanket hoping extra warmth will help.

Day 10 Empty Refrigerator

"So much for extra warmth. Muscles move. You are going to move. We have to go to the barn."

I put water on to heat and spoon some coffee into the strainer. "Just why am I trying to kill myself? If the place gets sold, that fence isn't going to matter. Where is that road crew? I need the electricity back on. I want a hot shower."

The water's hot. I pour it through the coffee grounds. "Coffee, make my day better." I sip some and feel the warmth spreading out. Caffeine chases the cobwebs out of my brain. "Time for chores."

This morning I round up the goats from the tree fallen near the chicken yard. "Forgot to close the gate last night." Herding unwilling goats is frustrating and hopeless. I go get a dish and feed. Two shakes and all the goats are in the barn.

By the time I let Gem and Jewel out, the barn is empty. They cry as they run out of the barn looking for their friends. All of them are working on the tree again when I let the chickens out of their house and put in feed and water. Arlo is lying nearby watching the chickens. "Chickens are off limits, Arlo."

Back in the house I get out the hamburger. The refrigerator smells funny. I prop the door open so the moisture will dry. The freezers need the same treatment.

When I open the container, the hamburger smells bad. That's the last of the freezer contents gone. I'm now on canned and sacked food. "Back to oatmeal for breakfast. Sassy, you're back to cat food."

Over breakfast I look at egg recipes in my cookbook. "Mostly omelets. Souffles and fritters require an oven I don't have. How did people make it without electricity at all? I sure miss it. Solar panels, why didn't we do solar panels, Justin?"

Walking down the road to the cow pasture, I can see down the fence line. A quarter of a mile is a long way. Starting at the gate I start counting posts again standing up. "One, two, three, four, five, six. This is stupid. Seven, eight, nine, ten, eleven, twelve, thirteen. At this rate, I'll take all year. Fourteen, fifteen, sixteen. Out of how many?"

Crossing the road so I can see, I count down to the first set of brace posts. There are twenty-one posts between where I've done and there. "I won't even make the first brace today. Maybe I'll give it up. Let the cows run all over. It's not like anyone can drive down here."

I can hear Justin. "The place is a dud. We need to sell."

"Selling isn't a bad idea. Being alone down here is stupid, asking for trouble. Except this is my place, my home. And I'm not going to drive any more."

"You loved driving. All you need is to start again. We can visit the national parks."

"No. I want a home and family. I want this place or one like it."

"You are my wife. You will do as I say."

I stare at the ground. I am his wife. According to my father, I will do as he tells me. The thought of driving, mostly at night down dark highways makes me shudder. The fence, the mindless routine of the fence shuts my mind off. Clear three sections. Push up and tap posts. Clear three sections. Push up and tap posts. Over and over. How many? I don't know. A hungry stomach interferes. Lunch time.

Standing in the kitchen I look around. "What do I eat? More oatmeal? Let's make some pancakes for bread. I must have something I can use for a sandwich."

The cookbook is still lying on the table. While the pancakes brown, I flip through the quick bread section. "Oven, oven, preheat oven. Spoon bread. Skillet. I'll have to try this. I think I have some corn meal in the cupboard."

Munching on a peanut butter and jelly pancake sandwich, I take a quick check on the goats, something to keep the brain occupied. They are still eating tree leaves. Let the chickens out. "Don't touch them, Arlo!" Back down the road to the fence. Back to the routine. Clear debris. Push and tap posts.

Big clouds are drifting overhead when I stop. It's late. Chore time. "Drat. There are only seven posts to the brace. I can't give up now. I have to. I'll be milking in the dark." I walk back carrying the tools to the house.

It's close to dark when I get back in from chores. Tonight I make sure all the gates are closed. The goats will be in the barn in the morning. I will cut branches in the morning so they have more to eat.

Scrambled eggs are dinner tonight along with boiled potato and canned peas. Baked potatoes are better, but no microwave, no oven. The potatoes are trying to sprout. I'm glad I didn't buy more than the one bag.

After dinner, I settle into my recliner. "Hey, where are the aches?" My muscles are stiff with a low level of complaint, but the pain is gone. "I'm getting tough. Ha! I can do it." On that note I dive into my thriller for a chapter or two before bed.

Day 11 Tractor Time

"Sassy, this is four days since the rain quit. Where is that road crew? I want my electricity back."

My cat ignores me. All she cares about right now is her food dish and kibble. I'm wondering how long before the kibble is gone. Maybe Sassy will make it on eggs and milk. We both might, if the road crew takes a couple of weeks to get here.

Milk turns sour in a day during August. Every morning and evening I dump what I had in the house and refill the bottle with fresh. It's a good thing I like my coffee black.

The goats are almost out of leaves around the yard. They wander out to the road and cross to the wet weather creek now a tame dribble. There are a down tree and several leaning ones to keep them busy for several days. The leaves are looking limp, but the goats still gobble them up.

Using my bow saw, I cut the top branches on the two trees the goats had been working on. It doesn't take long to put lots more leaves within reach. They will find them in the morning.

Humming some tune or medley of tunes I walk out to the cow pasture. "Seven posts and I'm to the first brace post. I am ready to be there."

After clearing the debris, I shove the first post. "What is with this? Move, post. There must be a rock."

The ground is firm. The muddy soil, soft and easy to push the posts in has dried into hard, wet soil. In sheer stubborn persistence I push two posts back up and tap them into place.

"The easy days are over. It's tractor time." I head back to the house for the key and the shed for the tractor. I open the door. A black snake streaks out and across the yard. I jump back gasping, my chest tight, my eyes wide.

"Black snakes are not poisonous. Black snakes eat mice. Why was it in there? Are there more?" I begin inspecting the ground around the tractor. No snakes.

The chain hangs from a big nail on one side of the tractor shed, barely within reach. "I was going to put a new one in, wasn't I? Where is my hammer and a nail?" I shove the chain off with a hoe. "I want to work on the fence. I'll put in a lower nail another day. No, I'll forget again." I put the new nail in, then take the chain to the tractor.

The tractor roars into life. It backs out into the mud. This is when those huge treads on big, back tractor tires really count as I drive across the yard toward the road leaving shallow ruts behind me.

Coming to the filled ditches along the culvert, I stop, get off and jump up and down on the fill I put in. It seems firm enough. "I'll have to trust it. I have to get to the cow pasture."

Climbing back up into the tractor seat, I put it back into gear. Taking a big breath, I start off and roll onto the debris. It holds. "Yay! We're across. Look out posts. Here we come."

We chug down the road along the cow pasture. The idea is to back the tractor up to the post, tie a chain between the tractor and post, ease the tractor forward and pull the post upright. I back up to the first post after the brace and turn the tractor off. Even the tractor won't get the posts up with all that debris on the wire. I spend the rest of the morning heaving debris off the wire.

Lunch is easy today as I made pancakes this morning. They don't make great bread slices, but they work. Sandwiches are so convenient for lunch, so portable. I wander out to check on the goats as I eat. They are still working on the leaves in the wet weather creek.

I wander down the road and back to the fence, the endless fence. I can see the next brace posts, but resist the urge to count the posts between me and them. I remind myself I've made it to the first set, a third of the way down this side.

"It only took three days to get this far. Let's see. There are three sections on the other side. That's nine days. There are two more sections here. Another six days. And two sections at each end for another twelve days totaling twenty-seven days, almost a month. And then there's the hay field."

I kick a stone down the road. "This is hopeless. I need help. And there isn't any help."

Wiping angry tears and blowing a drippy nose, I throw debris onto the road to the tune of "Justin, you fink. Justin, you liar. Mindy, you fool." until my arms give out. My back aches from bending over. It straightens up pulling at the muscles on both sides. Half this fence section is now close to empty of debris.

"Time to straighten a few posts." I tromp back to the tractor. Even the tractor can't straighten the posts with one try. I have to maneuver back and forth, but it stands up. The posts to the brace posts are up and I start down the next section.

Thunder breaks my concentration. I pound a last post, release the chain, set the sledge by my feet and chug my way down the road, through the gate and across to the cow barn. The tractor will be fine there for the night.

Drops are beginning to fall as I race toward the house. The goats are disappearing up the drive as I reach the road. I'm soaked by the time I reach the porch.

"Rain. Shower. Cold shower, but a shower." The clothes drop onto the mud porch floor. I grab a towel, soap and shampoo and head outside glad there's a short sidewalk out from the porch door.

The last of the shampoo washes out of my hair just before the thunderstorm moves on. It was surreal taking a bath with the lightning bursts and thunder. I know that's not a smart thing to do, but I haven't been clean in over a week. And it's so nice to be clean.

Sassy sneaks out of the closet when I go in for clean clothes. "Storm's over, Sassy. Time for chores. Do you want eggs for dinner?"

Walking to the barn I see the rain has filled the rain barrels. I put hay out in the barn. It has little appeal for the goats. Grain, those tasty to them morsels, have the six crowding the door. "You gluttons, you can hardly get through the door you're so full of leaves."

Once facing a dish of grain, they play with the oats. Shove it one way. Shove it the other way. Crunch a few.

Tonight I can easily get done milking and take to pushing the goats out the door before they finish their grain.

"You'll be there all night playing with your food. Maybe you'll be hungry in the morning." I close the gate on my way back to the house.

Sassy noses the scrambled eggs and begs for kibble. "You're in trouble, when the crunchies are gone." I put some kibble in her dish. My scrambled eggs are good with fried potatoes and canned peas.

Pages turn in my thriller. The pieces are coming together. Tomorrow night will be the end of this book and I'll tackle some of the ones I bought.

Day 12 Can't Never did Anything

I lie in bed watching light creep into the room. It's been almost a week since the rain stopped. Maybe the road crew will get here in another day or two. And Justin will follow the road crew. What then? I don't know. I need to know. Later, I'll decide later. I stretch and find my muscles are stiff. "At least they don't hurt. Sassy, it's time for me to get up."

Waiting for water to heat, I look at the briefcase. "I wonder how hard selling this place will be. Mrs. Watson didn't say how long it took her. Maybe we were the only people dumb enough to get out of the car and look the place over. Selling is the smart thing to do. I can't take care of the place by myself. If we do sell it, where will I go?"

Expresso coffee wakes me up. "Justin wants me to drive again. Will he let me live someplace else? Will he force me to drive? Will I let him? What if I stay here? What can he do about it? I wish I could talk to someone, get some ideas. I can't. So, what do I want to do?" The mug goes back on the sink and I head out the door to milk.

Detouring to the end of the yard looking over the road, I can see the cow pasture fence. Even with Justin here, that fence took over a month to put up. "I am a fool to think I can take care of this place by myself. Can't do it."

My grandmother had an opinion on that. She was teaching me to sew a button on and I'd tangled the thread yet again. "Can't never did anything." It took another try or two, but I got that button sewed on.

"I can do it, Grandmother. I just need help." A lot of help. I need Justin. Justin's not here. He lied to me. He left. He won't come back except to sell my home. Even if I am an idiot to stay here alone, it is home. And I am alone."

I trudge up to the barn. Chores need to get done. The fence needs to get done. What I wouldn't give for a day in town.

The goats have found the limbs I cut. I have to drag them in and they are eager to get done. The leaves won't last long, so I leave the barn lot gate open. They can check out the other tree for those leaves, then head across the road and down the wet weather creek. They won't need the hill pasture for another week or more. The cows will need their pasture soon.

The cheese will last the day, so I only need milk for the day. I hate to keep dumping it out. Maybe the chickens would like it. I take an old pan out, put it in the chicken yard and pour milk into it.

My flock inspects this new offering. Cheese, they know and love. This isn't cheese. A brave hen tries some. And the competition begins. Milk is popular.

Sassy meows hello as I walk up to the house. I put a taste of milk down for her. She takes a lap or two and wanders off. Pancakes for breakfast again.

As the cakes cook, I look at the briefcase again. Justin will disappear with it as soon as he can. That will leave me with no way to prove he has been lying to me. Tonight, I will sort out some papers and stash them. My life, my marriage is blowing up in my face. Does he love me enough to admit his lies, to try to rebuild my trust in him?

I pick up the phone. It's still dead. I need to talk to someone. Maybe Justin can explain. Mostly I want to hear someone's voice. The solitude here is wonderful, but I want company too.

It's time to tackle the fence again. I walk over to the cow barn to get the tractor. "Let's take a look at the hay. If it's ruined, it is. I should find out."

The sandbag feed sacks pull away from the door. I open the door. The floor is wet. A muddy line is a few inches up on the walls so the bottom bales are ruined. The rest may be fine. "All that work paid off." I leave the doors propped open to let the floor dry out.

The tractor chugs its way back to the road and down the fence. On the way I admire the part again standing. Then the line waiting stretches out. I back the tractor up to the next post and turn the key off.

I stand staring up the fence line. "Forget this. There's no way I can get this done without help. What's the point, if we're going to sell the place? The cows can wander up the road. They can't get far. And no one's going to be driving down here."

The fence needs doing. "The only help you can count on is at the end of your arm," said my mother. She first told me that when my school project partner suddenly moved away leaving me the only one doing the project. I was whining to her hoping she would talk to my teacher. She refused. I could do it, she said. I need help I told her.

"My mother is right. I can't depend on Justin. He's gone. My help is the hand at the end of my arm. Those posts won't stand up by themselves. The cows need their pasture. Let's get that stuff off the wire."

Sheer stubbornness keeps me tossing debris off the wire until my back screams it's time to stop. I stretch the muscles, rub them to get the pain out. Five more sections will take me to the next brace posts. "Come on, back. Only five more."

According to my back, those five will have to wait until later. I'll straighten posts until my back eases off. Settled into the seat, I touch the key and stop. "Is that a helicopter? Probably Air Evac taking someone to St. Louis. It's coming right over the house." I get off the tractor and go out in the pasture for a better look. It's only a machine, but it's my first glimpse of people in days.

The helicopter swings out over the pasture and settles down. A man gets out. I wait.

"Mike Bremmer. FEMA. We're out checking on all the houses, checking on people. Didn't expect to see anyone down here. Are you the only one here? Did anyone get hurt?"

"I'm the only one here. I'm doing all right. Phone is out. Electricity is out. The road's a mess. Water supply is running low. When will the road crew get here?"

"They might get here in a couple of weeks, but not likely. The whole county is like here, even worse. Lots of trees down. I counted at least seven on this road as we flew down."

"I won't make it a couple of weeks. I've got animal feed for that long, maybe. But the water I put up in the house will be gone in a week. I'm using the tractor and will need diesel."

"What about food?"

"The refrigerator and freezers are empty. I have canned stuff. I have milk and eggs."

"I've got a couple of gallons of water I can leave now. Let me call in about your phone. Trees fell on some phone posts so rain got in, shorted them out."

"There's no cell signal down here," I tell Mike when he takes his out of his pocket.

"You're right. Well, write down the information and I'll call it in later."

I take the notebook and pen to write down about my phone. Mike's looking down the fence line. "You did that? Alone?"

"Yes."

"Not many women could do that. Or would. I'll make sure more water gets here in a couple of days. I don't know if I can carry diesel. I'll find out and let you know when I bring the water. We'll check in once a week until you're able to get out."

"Thanks. It's nice to see someone."

"See you in a few days." Mike gets back in the helicopter, brings out three jugs of water, gets back in and the copter's gone.

I stand watching the copter fly off, remain there listening to it. Being alone had seemed almost normal. Now I wish I could go to town or call someone so much it hurts. Grabbing two jugs of water, I walk back to the house for lunch.

"It's not that you're not good company, Sassy. The problem is conversation. I can talk to you, the goats and the chickens. Even Arlo likes to listen to me, I think. But none of you can really answer me."

I find my jelly supply is running low. What can I replace peanut butter and jelly sandwiches with for lunch? "Being stuck here for weeks is no fun at all. Sassy, even you will be unhappy if I can't get you more kibble. And I need to talk to the bank about the joint account. We're stuck for at least two more weeks. What am I going to do?"

Fix fence. And I'm back at it after lunch. All the debris is off to the next brace posts. I start in pulling up posts.

Lengthening shadows remind me I need to do chores before dark. I'm only half way to the brace posts, but it won't take long in the morning to straighten the rest of the posts. The tractor spends the night in the cow barn.

The goats ignore their hay. They play with their grain. Milking goes fast. Tonight, I dump it in a bucket for Arlo as I'm tired and the chickens are going to bed. It disappears. I wonder how long his food will last. The eggs are a bit muddy again after yesterday's storm. The filled rain barrels will keep the animals' water filled, the toilet and some for washing off eggs and my face. August storms usually come once a week, so they may be all right.

Dinner is scrambled eggs, boiled potatoes and corn. It's not a bad dinner, easy to fix by candlelight. "I hope the candle supply holds out another couple of weeks. The electricity won't be on before the road is fixed. Maybe I'll start only lighting one each night. Maybe I'll buy a couple of camping lanterns next time I get to town. If I ever get to town. Sassy, I hate to admit it, but Justin has a point. Getting stranded for weeks is no fun. Maybe I should sell, find a better place closer to town."

Setting the briefcase down, I open it. Justin lied, that's fact. Would he lie to me now? What is certain is, if I take papers out of the briefcase, I'm expecting him to keep lying. And my marriage will end. Am I ready to do that? I close the briefcase and set it back.

I settle into my recliner. The thriller is heating up. It will be a late night as I want to finish it tonight. The candle is only a stub when I close the cover.

"Maybe Mike can return my library books. I'll have to ask."

Day 13 Paper Insurance

The sun is up when I wake up. My head feels heavy. Even coffee doesn't help much. I drag out to the barn.

Goats spot all opportunities. Sleepy milkers are an opportunity for extra feed I can't afford to give them. Precious bumps into the dog food bucket spilling some out. It disappears down goat gullets. Hay gets knocked down my collar by goats standing up demanding I hurry up.

By the time I get to the chicken house, I'm fuming. Chickens stuck in the doorway don't help. A filthy water fount is worse as I miscalculate and spill the water down my jeans into my boot.

The pancakes burn when I fall asleep cooking them. I'm out of syrup and can't find more in the pantry. There should be more. There isn't. I use cheese as I want the jelly for lunch. Cheese doesn't work on pancakes when my mouth is primed for syrup.

My head demands more sleep. The cow pasture fence demands fixing and all I have to do is pull posts up and secure them all the way to the brace posts. I go out to fix fence.

Driving across to the fence my mind wanders. My eyes are heavy. I back up and semi fall off to put the chain on the first post. The tractor seat seems such a pull away. I ease the tractor forward.

"Ow!" My brain snaps awake as the chain pelts my leg and crashes into the side of the tractor. "What happened?" I shake my head trying to clear sleepy fog out. "I put the chain on the post and pulled with the tractor. And fell asleep. And didn't stop."

I ease the tractor back, put the chain back on and the post eases back to upright. A couple of taps with the sledge hammer to secure it. Ease the tractor back and turn it off. Take the chain off.

"I'll have a dandy bruise. This isn't the place to be. Nap time." And asleep is what I stay until lunch time.

A tiny fleck of mold is on the lip of the jar of jelly. I scrape the mold off and slather jelly onto the peanut butter on the pancake. There's one more jar in the pantry. "I suppose I could have cheese sandwiches for lunch. The ricotta, if I drain it well, does slice."

Sandwich eaten, I go back to the cow pasture and that line of fence posts. This time I'm awake and the posts go up fast or seem to. By chore time I've straightened posts to the second brace posts. One more stretch, another two or three days, and one side of the pasture will be up. I might even finish the pasture by the time the road crew shows up.

Walking back from parking the tractor I detour over to walk along the repaired fence. "It would go up so much faster if Justin was here. Two of us could make the place pay its way, especially if we'd bought that other place, put some cattle on it. And we could have, if he'd put in money too."

My shoulders sag. Justin's not here. He won't come back. If I'm honest, I can't run the place alone. I'll have to give it up. "We worked so hard. I'm still working hard. And he wants to throw it all away. Take my home away. Make me drive again. No, I won't drive again whether I stay here or not. I've got to put those papers aside tonight."

Scattering grain in the chicken yard, I call my little flock in. They crowd around my feet pecking up the grain. There are a dozen hens and seven eggs are in the nests. They will make sure I have food to eat. I hope I can keep feeding them until the road is cleared.

I check the garden on my way back to the barn. The radishes are spreading their little seed leaves. In a month I'll be munching on radishes. I go on to look over my orchard. Tonight I will have my own Red Delicious apples for dessert.

Putting hay out in the goat barn I stop to scratch Precious' itchy spot at the base of her neck. Her neck arcs up and her eyes half close as she leans into my fingers. Where will we go? Justin will send them to the sale barn. They are just animals to him, animals he cares nothing about. Does he care about me?

Oatmeal works for dinner. I need to use up the raisins before they mold. How did people keep food before refrigerators? Maybe they just ate differently.

After cleaning up, I open the briefcase. Those neat little files of papers sit in their folders. Bombs blowing up my life.

"He'll notice anything missing from this year. I'll get some from last year. A couple of months of brokerage reports, a couple of months of savings statements should be enough. And I want the deed for the property, my property."

I thumb through the papers in the top file. There's the property deed. I put it aside. There are the powers of attorney. I take out mine. How do I cancel it? Why do I want Justin, my lying husband, to have power of attorney over me? Next is my birth certificate. And the title to my truck. "Now, what do I do with them?"

All the remaining papers are arranged in the briefcase. It's closed. I take it back to the closet and set it back where I found it.

"Where do I put my papers? He'll recognize them, if he sees them." I fold the papers and stash them in my cookbook. Justin will never look in it.

Trust is the basis of a marriage. Justin lied to me. Now I'm deceiving him. Where does it end? "Justin, will you tell me the truth? I don't want to lose you."

Another hour is spent trying to get interested in another thriller. I give up and curl up around Sassy in bed only to wake with nightmares of driving down endless dark tunnels lit with headlights before dawn lets me crawl out to start another day.

Day 14 Comparing Dreams

"Sassy, I might get to liking this coffee method in another week or two. I'm not flipping light switches now. This is scary. No electricity is becoming normal. I still miss it."

The goats are awake and eager to eat. I put out some hay and start milking. The room is still dim. The oat barrel is low. I grab the next bag and start to drag it over. A line of oats forms a trail behind the bag.

"Mice. I have some traps somewhere." The barrel holds all but one sack. "I'll feed out of this one, get it emptied."

After milking, I dump chicken scratch and egg crumbles in their barrels. The scratch bag also has little holes in it. "Drat. I hate to set mouse traps. But, if the place is full of mice, snakes will move in. Maybe I should start putting out range cubes for the steers again."

Mixing pancakes, I find the flour is running low. "So much for sandwiches. But I'm almost out of jelly anyway. I wonder if Mike would do some shopping for me. It's been a couple of days and he said he'd be back. I wonder what day it is. I'll have to ask."

Eating breakfast, I look over at my cookbook. "I wonder how long he was going to keep lying to me. Why did he lie? Can I ever trust him again?"

If we'd really been partners here, if he'd really wanted the place to work, we'd have a generator or solar panels. He'd be here to help. That was my dream. "What was his dream? I guess I don't know. Strange, since we've been married almost eleven years. It seems we don't really know each other. The fence is waiting."

Starting up the tractor I check the gas gauge. The tractor is really good about using diesel, but it's down a quarter. I won't have enough to do the whole pasture, if I use the tractor for all of the posts.

"Road crew, I need you. Mike said seven trees across the road. Even if I could use the chainsaw, I'd never clear all of them."

This is the last section on this side. I start throwing debris off the wire. Grab. Toss. Grab. Toss. Occasional branches must be dug and pulled free. The back cramps.

Now the tractor pulls up the first post. Tap it into place. Move on to the next one. Tap it. Do a third. Go back to the first one. Repeat.

By lunch time six posts are standing up. I walk back to the house. Sandwich in hand, I check on the goats now down to the creek and walk back across the pasture.

More debris tossed. More posts straightened. Now it's time for chores. Another exciting day is closing down with me still not quite halfway to the corner posts.

I have to go down to the creek and chase the goats up to the barn. It's still light and they are still eating. Convincing reluctant goats to go somewhere is infuriating as they scatter, turn back, ignore me then act like I'm a monster chasing them and stampede up to the barn.

I stomp up through the mud and water still running down the wet weather creek. "Those stupid goats deserve the sale barn. If I got rid of them, I could go wherever I wanted. I wouldn't be stuck fixing that stupid fence." I fling open the milk room door. "Precious, get in here."

Six goats stand staring at me. I step out. A chorus of snorts is left behind as they take off into the barn lot. I slam the door closed and head for the chickens.

Half the chickens come running for their grain. The other half ignores me. I round them up finding they don't stay together, but wander off in separate directions. Once I round up all the strays, I gather the eggs. "The eggs are great. Are they worth this?" I stomp off to the house.

"More eggs for dinner. Pretty soon I'll be having eggs three times a day."

After leaving the eggs in the kitchen, I go back out to the barn. It's starting to get dark. The goats are back in the barn. I put out hay which they ignore. Scratching Precious over her shoulders seems to be an apology in her opinion. She leads the others over to the milk room door. It's almost full night by the time I finish and grope my way back to the house.

The last of the potatoes joins my eggs for dinner. Tonight, I splurge with some chocolate in a glass of milk. It might be better hot, but it's good warm too. I want my refrigerator back. I want the lights on. What I wouldn't give for a hot shower.

How much longer before the road crew gets here? What about the electric crew? Can I make it that long here alone? Right now, I'd even settle for talking to Justin. I pick up the phone. Nothing.

The new thriller still doesn't interest me much. I sort through the stack I'd bought at that book sale and pick out an historical fiction I bought on a whim. It would be different.

Soon I'm moving across the plains in a covered wagon on my way to Oregon. My troubles pale to nothing compared to those of this family. Unlike them, I have a house, livestock and relative safety. All I lack is a companion.

Day 15 Losing Dreams

Before heading to the kitchen, I open the briefcase and take out our marriage certificate. I set it on the kitchen table. Justin is my husband. He is supposed to be my companion. Or is it the other way around? Or are we partners?

"I guess Justin and my father think alike. A wife obeys her husband no matter what. That means the place gets sold, the animals get sold. I go back to driving." I shudder at the thought of driving again. Sassy rubs against my ankles.

"Sassy, Justin says you go to the shelter, the goats and steers go to the sale barn. And I go back to driving a truck, something I hate to do now. He's my husband and I'm supposed to do as he says, no matter what. Do you agree? The shelter is curtains for you. The sale barn is the end for the goats. Driving is the end of me."

Gulping down my coffee, I pick up my bucket and tote to go to the barn. Dawn's chill is still in the air. Clouds are blue with pink starting to light them up. In the barn I hear the goats starting to get up. "How do I give this up? How do I stuff this down into a fond memory? Can I force myself to drive again?"

The goats are wary of me as I milk with tears streaming down my cheeks. They suffer being hugged as they go back into the barn. Hay dust makes me sneeze making my nose run even more. Life without this place looks empty. Life on the place looks dismal.

Breakfast is oatmeal, a batch big enough to make lunch too. I walk to the cow pasture and can't go in. Instead, I walk down the road, clamber through the fallen tree I wish hadn't been there to catch me and down the road. Pipe dreams of what I hoped was the future fill my head.

Justin and I working as a team, making the place a showcase. Slipping around the gate posts and staring off across the overgrown pastures of the place past mine I see green grass dotted with cows and calves. Tears start again trying to ease the ache filling me.

"Why did you lie to me? Why did you let me hold on to a dream, realize a dream you didn't want and planned to destroy? How long were you going to keep lying to me? I believed you and saw nothing except what you let me see, what I wanted to see. Can I pretend everything is like it was? Can I forgive? I don't know. Do I want to try? I don't know."

An overgrown driveway stretches out in front of me. Leaving the gateposts behind, I follow it up a slope. A few branches and a couple of small fallen trees lie across it. Stepping over them I look over the pastures to my right. Debris sits on top of the brush down near the creek. I recognize the multiflora roses grown to huge masses. Lots of red cedars reach up through the bushes. Hills are on the other side of where the creek is although I can't see it.

More pastures are on my left. Wood fence posts lean or lie flat, the attached wire rusty. Goats would love this mess.

The drive rises up and loops through a group of pines. Following the loop, I can see the house. It looks like a farmhouse, the kind I remember in books I read growing up. It's rectangular with a steep roof broken by two gables looking at me.

Several of the windows are broken. A limb from the large pine standing in front of the house broke off and dented the brown metal roof. It's still sitting in the dent so I can't tell if there's a hole in the roof or not. An electric pole stands at one end of the yard, away from the pines, so the house had electricity at one time.

Staring at the house with its abandoned, derelict look I find it matches the feeling inside me. I turn and walk away more quickly than I came trying to outrun the sadness, the despair that permeates the place. Or is it the sadness inside me that I'm trying to outrun?

I walk back to the mindless repetition of straightening the fence. Lunchtime comes and goes. Lengthening shadows and reaching the corner posts finally make me quit.

After milking, I eat the oatmeal I'd planned to eat at noon. Warm milk warms it up a little. The dark house wraps around me like a comforting blanket. "Tonight is made for a thrilling movie. I guess a book will have to do."

Sassy curls up in my lap as I go back on the journey over the Oregon Trail.

Day 16 Helicopter Bringing Water

"I finished one side, Sassy. It's probably a waste of time, but I'll start on the far end today."

My water supply is down to a couple of jugs. I make coffee. "Mike better come back soon. The creek water may look clear again, but it's full of leaves and fish and other stuff. I guess I'd have to boil it a half hour or more. Maybe I could use the pressure canner. I need to make out a shopping list."

When I look on the table, the marriage certificate is lying there. I pick it up and walk back into the bedroom to the briefcase. "It's back with the other lying papers. I wonder if our marriage is one of his lies." I close the briefcase and set it back in the closet.

Dawn is lighting the clouds with deep salmon pink as I walk to the barn. It's a color no artist can ever duplicate with its deep glow. "It's going to be a good day."

Chores go quickly. The goats happily race off down the wet weather creek to the creek bed. "You are going to be so unhappy stuck in the hill pasture once I get those cows moved." If they hear, they don't understand.

Another jug of water is empty after I make oatmeal. Even cut with milk, it takes water. Straight milk scorches to the bottom of the pan and is murder to scrape off. I'll do pancakes again tomorrow even though the flour is running out.

The first snag of the day comes when I drive the tractor up to the end fence and find all the posts are leaning into the field. I can't use the tractor to push them up. The come-along is hanging in the tractor shed so I take the tractor back to the barn and walk over to the shed to get it.

A come-along is designed to pull barbed wire tight. You hook the come-along to something solid like a rope around a tree, hook the wire to the other end and pull the lever over and over to rachet up the slack. I'm going to put a chain over each post top and rachet up the slack to pull the post back up.

The only thing fast about fixing fence this morning is throwing the debris off the wire. In frustration I take to pulling the second post down upright, pushing the first one up and trying to tap it in while pushing and trying not to miss the post as that might leave me with a broken arm. Sledge hammers are heavy and would snap bone, if I hit one by mistake.

"Doing this alone is stupid. Being down here alone is stupid. What do I do, if I get hurt? No one will get here to find me. Maybe this place is a dud. Maybe I need a different place I can handle alone. Maybe I just need a real partner who wants to be here."

By the time my stomach announces lunch, I have seven posts standing up and three pretending. At this rate it will take me as long to do this short end fence as it did to do the road fence. I leave the tools where they are and start the trek back to the house.

"The helicopter! I hear it." I stand out in the pasture trying to spot it. The sound bounces between the hills. It appears over the hill in the direction of town.

I wave and move over toward the fence to give the helicopter room to land. It settles onto the pasture and Mike climbs out carrying some jugs of water. "How's it going?"

"I have one side done. It's slow."

"You still have enough food?"

"I'm running low on flour, oatmeal and cat food. I'm glad to see the water as I'm down to one gallon in the house."

"I checked and I can't bring diesel out."

"Not a problem. I have to use a come-along now. The posts are leaning the wrong way for the tractor. How's the road crew doing?"

"They're working north of town. It's a shame you can't cut some of this up from here."

"There is a chainsaw, but it's too big for me to use. I guess there are more people living along those roads."

"True. You are the only one down here and you don't have any medical emergency needs. If you did, I'd probably fly you out."

"I'll need feed in a little over a week."

"I can't bring that out either. Only food and water for you. I'll try to include some cat food. Dry stuff?"

"That would do fine. I'll cut back on the feed, try to stretch it."

"Is the phone working again?"

"Don't think so. I haven't checked it today."

"Those crews are having to replace lots of posts too. I brought out a couple of local papers so you can see what the storm did around here."

"My first news in a couple of weeks. What day is it anyway? I lost track ages ago."

"This is Monday, the twenty-third."

"Monday. I'll have to make a note. One day is pretty much like any other here. All I seem to do is work on that fence."

Mike takes out a notebook. "Now, you said you need flour, oatmeal."

"The old fashioned kind and cat kibble. Maybe a small bottle of syrup. It doesn't keep long without the refrigerator."

"Those crews are working north of town too, following the road crews. Lots of poles got snapped when trees fell on the lines."

"The poles here are out in the pastures. I don't think any are broken in the field up from me. I was down that way looking over the fences. Found a cow tangled in the barbed wire and cut her loose. I have some cows and calves from there here with my steers."

"Anything else?"

"Coffee. I'm making expresso with the coffeemaker stuff. Maybe potatoes, some canned vegetables. A loaf of bread, peanut butter and jelly, small jars as it doesn't keep long either."

"No guarantees. I'll see what I can do and be back about Friday. Otherwise, it will be Monday. I'll leave more water."

When Mike and the helicopter fly off, I have a dozen jugs of water to cart back to the house. I grab two on my way to get some lunch, one in each hand and the papers stuck in my belt.

The oatmeal for lunch goes down a spoonful at a time as I browse my way through the papers. I measured fifty-eight inches. Officially the storm dropped fifty-five. Eight people were confirmed dead with another twenty missing. If that tree hadn't caught me, I would be among the missing.

Pictures of the damage in town make here look untouched. Trees smashing roofs, broken electric poles, washed out roads, cars half covered with water, I stare at the damage. No wonder the road crews won't get here for weeks along with the electric crews. There's mention of tremendous damage all along the storm's path so crews coming from other areas and states are spread thin.

"Well, Sassy, we're going to be here a while. Maybe I'll plant the fall garden this afternoon. I could use a break from the fence."

On the way out of the house, I check the phone. Still dead.

Ever the optimist in the garden, I prepare and sow seeds for spinach, turnips, more lettuce, winter radishes, bok choi, Napa cabbage, beets and mizuna. When I get to town, if I ever get to town again, I'll get some cabbage transplants. These will probably need row covers to protect from insects and frost before they are ready to harvest, but I do love fresh greens as long as possible.

There's still a couple of hours left before chore time. I go back to the cow pasture fence. Every post is a victory. Every post gets me closer to moving those cows back here. And the grass is recovering from the flood so there will be plenty for them to eat.

I carry more jugs of water back to the house after putting things up in the barn. The tractor can stay in the cow barn for now. The tools will be needed again tomorrow.

The goats are still out along the creek after I get the chickens back in their pen. A trip down to the cow pasture lets me pick up a couple more jugs of water. Calling the goats gets their attention. Precious leads the group back up the wet weather creek, across the road and up to the barn. I detour by the house to leave the water.

Sunset is painting the sky when I finish milking. I set the milk down on the kitchen counter, then walk down to the cow pasture. Deep shadows darken the pasture. A snort and white tail bounding across the grass startle me. Several more white tails are visible as deer take off for the creek. I grab two more jugs of water wishing I could carry more, but two gallons of water are heavy and seem to gain weight during the walk back to the house.

I light a candle so I can see to scramble some eggs and heat some canned peas for dinner. Losing all my frozen produce will make slim pickings for cooking this winter. And I can't replace it as the deer ate my tomato and pepper plants along with taking bites out of the squash. There are some more squash growing on the vines. I'll have to check on them tomorrow.

After another hour spent on the Oregon Trail, Sassy and I stretch out in bed. Dawn comes early.

Day 17 Cow Refugees

My muscles stretch and relax pulling me back to sleep blurring the grey light in the window. I'm in a cattle drive surrounded by mooing cows. Cows? I sit up. That mooing is no dream.

Looking out in the yard I see big shapes walking around. What are the cows doing in my yard? How did they get out of the hill pasture? The two gates, one to the road and one to the bridge, are closed.

Hastily I pull on clothes wishing I could do a load of laundry. Washing out underwear does clean it, but leaves it stiff and scratchy. Stumbling out to the mud porch, I pull on my boots and go out the door. "What are you doing here, cows? Get out of my yard. Shoo! Scram! Get down that driveway now!"

The cows meander down the yard. There are no steers. These are not from the hill pasture. They are from down the road. I don't need more cows. I need fences fixed.

I count a dozen, more or less, with some calves. They go across the road and into the hay field. Grass is growing there too. I close the driveway gate.

"Where's the coffee? I'm awake. I want my coffee." Soon water is heating on the stove. I'm assembling my bucket and tote. Sassy is still puffed up and checking out the window sills. She ignores her kibble.

My goats are standing in the barn door, tails and backbone fur standing. I call Precious and get answered with snorts. She slides away from my hand. I drag Priscilla into the milk room. That gets Precious in too.

When I walk over to the chicken yard, the goats are standing at the top of the driveway looking over at the hay field. The group is still there when I walk back to the barn. I walk down to open the gate. No one wants to go out. I close the gate and lead the goats back to the big oak and another tree at the end of the yard. Breakfast is next on my list.

An hour later, with ricotta setting up in a pot and breakfast eaten, I go back to the driveway gate to find the goats milling around. This time I go out the gate and they follow me. I take them down the road to the fallen tree by the fence I'm working on.

Post by post this fence gets cleaned off, pulled up and tapped into place. It's going faster than yesterday, but still slower than the other fence line. By lunch I'm four posts from the first brace posts although another three aren't quite straight yet.

The bow saw comes back with me after lunch. I cut some tall branches on the fallen tree for the goats. There's a limb on the fence. I cut it and toss it over into the trees.

By chore time I've passed the brace posts by five posts with two more part way up. I take the tools over to the barn, walk down the road and call the goats. They walk back with me. We go in the driveway gate and I close it. No cows are welcome in the yard. They are still over in the hay field.

Chickens secured in their house, goats nosing hay in their barn, steers and cows happily vying for range cubes, I head for the house. Another candle burns as I fix dinner, more eggs and canned veggies. Sassy and I are half way to Oregon when we crawl into bed.

Day 18 Frustration

I lie awake under the sheet pulled over me. Mornings are cooler now. Dawn is starting. I sit up and start getting dressed. Quiet descends and surrounds me. No electricity. No lights. I'm running out of candles. I want a shower. I want my refrigerator. I want my coffeemaker. I get up.

The phone is sitting in its cradle. Dead. I want to call someone, talk to someone, even Justin.

"Hello, Justin. How are things for you? I'm still stuck here. You're right, being stuck is awful. The storm didn't do much damage here, mostly the fences. Why didn't we buy a generator? We could have put up solar panels. Why did you lie to me?"

I toss kibble in Sassy's dish. She goes back to the bedroom. The water is hot and I pour it through the coffee grounds. Coffee will make me feel better. I burn my tongue.

Pictures of storm damage stare at me from the papers lying on the table. The flood was awful here, but the damage was minimal in comparison to town. None of my roofs blew off or had trees fall on them. Maybe this isn't such a bad place. "Yeah, right. No phone, no electricity, can't get out, no help. It's a great place, if no storms come by or you own a helicopter."

Slamming the porch screen and stomping across to the barn don't help the dead feeling on my tongue. Being mad at the goats won't help. I slam the bucket and tote down on the table and walk out on the step.

Deep breaths. Watch the sunrise colors. Feel the coolness. Yes, a place closer to town would be nice, but those places got wiped out by the storm. Yes, having someone else here for company would be nice. It won't happen. "Either I stay here alone or I sell out, if I can, and join Justin driving. I'll stay here." I shrug and go back into the milk room.

How much is in the feed barrels? What am I going to do? The road crew won't be coming for at least another week, probably longer. The steers are the only ones with extra feed because I didn't take anything over to them during the storm or several days after. The oat barrel is a full, but the extra bag is gone. I'll cut the goats to half. What about the chickens? They'll have to get less too. Even so, the feed will be gone in another week.

If I stay here, I'll need to find a job. Maybe I can do deliveries for some company or store in town. I'm a good driver. I just don't want to go on those long hauls again.

What about Justin? Can he make me sell the place? Who would buy it? Some city people wanting a hunting camp? Where would I move? Would he let me use the money to buy another place? It would be my money. I paid for this place.

Anger again fills me. "No good thinking about it. Let it go. You're stuck here. There's nothing you can do. Let it go. Get the chores done. You've got fence to fix."

The goats eye me warily. I snap at them. They finish eating their half rations long before I finish milking. Topaz kicks the bucket spilling milk across the stand and I explode. She cowers under my screams. I burst into tears and hug her. She shivers in my arms, bolting out the door when I open it.

Gem and Jewel mouth their grain watching me. They relax by the time I finally get done milking. My anger is gone, washed away by my tears.

After breakfast, I go back to that endless fence. It isn't really endless, it just feels that way. I stare down the short side I'm working on. I won't make the second set of brace posts today. Tomorrow. Maybe three days to finish this side.

"Won't get done, if I don't get to work." I attach the come-along to a tree and the chain over a post. Stand it up. Push up the post before this one. Pound it into place. Pound this post in. Let the come-along loose. Move up two posts. Repeat. Repeat.

Lunch time finds me half way to the next brace posts. Chore time finds me five posts from the brace posts. I'll be on to the next section tomorrow.

Chores get done. Another candle is lit. I count. Ten more candles in the box. After that, I guess I cook in the dark and go to bed with the chickens. But tonight I still have light to get back on the Oregon Trail for a time before crawling into bed wishing I could take a bath, wash some clothes, feel clean. Maybe it will rain soon.

Day 19 The Phone: Two-Edged Sword

Another cool morning greets me. Fall is dropping hints. Hot coffee warms my insides. This morning I'm careful as my tongue reminds me of yesterday's assault.

The goats are up and playing when I get to the barn. They are impatient with half rations, but I hold firm. The feed will be gone soon enough as it is. The last of the dogfood goes into Arlo's feeder. He gets most of the milk.

The last of the flour goes into pancakes for breakfast. I spread one with jelly to eat now. That jar will be empty after lunch. Mike said he'd try to bring some food on the next trip. If he doesn't, I'll be living on fried eggs, milk and oatmeal. Even that won't be for long as the oatmeal is close to gone too.

"I need to get to town, Sassy. You will be out of food soon too. And you don't like eggs."

August sun is warming the day up nicely as I walk back across the cow pasture. "I'll be done with two sides tomorrow night. Not bad. Maybe I can do the other short side next and move the cows back over next week."

By lunch time I've passed the brace posts and started down the last section. Back at the house I settle into a chair to rest as I eat this last pancake sandwich. "Eggs for lunch tomorrow and dinner tonight. That's right, there's a squash or two to pick."

I walk out to the garden and check on my lettuce seeds. The first ones are peeking out of the soil. Two squash are ready. I clip them off with the pruners and take them back to the house.

"What's that? The phone!" I race into the house and pounce on the phone. "Hello? Hello?"

"Hello. I'm from the phone company. Your phone is fixed. Sorry it took so long."

"This is wonderful. Thank you so much."

"Have a good afternoon."

The man hangs up. I push the button and the dial tone sounds. Who will I call first?

"I better pay the phone bill first."

Five minutes later the bill is paid. Next, I call the sheriff's office and ask about who is renting the place up from mine explaining about the cows. They refer me to a real estate office to find out who is handling the rental. It turns out to be the right place and they will relay the message.

I put down the phone. There is another call to the bank. I look up the number and call. "Hello, I wanted to check the balance in my account."

"No, I'm not online. And my electricity is out."

I read them the account number and verify I'm who I say I am with other information.

"One hundred dollars? There should be twenty thousand. Are you sure?"

"Transferred yesterday? I'll bet it was to a St. Louis bank, right?"

"Thanks." I set the phone down. Justin emptied my account. Even if I get to town, I can't buy anything. A hundred dollars will cover the phone bill and a little food. No feed. No gas. What am I going to do? What is he trying to do? "That's my money he stole. And he's in town. At least he can't get out here." My brain goes numb. "He took twenty thousand dollars." I'm walking back to the fence. "What am I going to do? It's my money and he just took it, put it in that secret account. The louse. He's going to give it back. I'll find a way to make him pay it back. I need that money to stay here."

Every post is a way to strangle Justin. Every blow with the sledge hammer is on his head. That money was enough to keep me for over two years, long enough to find a job and get on my feet here so I wouldn't have to sell.

"That's why he took the money. Now I have to sell. He may force me to sell, but he can't force me to drive again. Why would I want to be his partner? Why do I want to be his wife?"

It's close to dark before I notice. I leave the tools where they are and run for the house. I'll be milking in the dark.

Milking by flashlight is not recommended. It throws strange shadows on the walls. The goats are convinced monsters are hiding in every single one. They don't notice the short rations as they stare around the milk room and slither back out into the barn.

Back in the house I light another candle. Fresh squash tastes great. Sitting at the table the enormity of being totally broke seeps in through the anger that has cooled.

"What am I going to do? I need feed and that's not cheap. I can't run a bill. Lee would let me, but I can't pay it later. What am I going to do?"

There's the electric bill to pay. It won't be much, mostly the basic fee. But it is a bill.

"I need a job. What can I do? Drive. That's what I'm good at. I could deliver pizzas. Who else uses drivers? I don't know. Who can I ask?"

Sassy settles into my lap. I open my book and stare at the page. I close the book and scoop Sassy up to hug her. "We're in trouble, Sassy. You're in trouble. The goats are in trouble. What am I going to do? Maybe I can sell some of the steers. I won't get as much selling early, but it will be cash. And I can't keep the money to buy more next spring."

The phone rings. I wait for the answering machine to pick up. It doesn't. No electricity. No answering machine. I get up and walk over to stare at the phone.

It's Justin. I know it's Justin. No one else would be calling me now. And I don't want to talk to him.

Finally, the phone stops ringing. I reach over and pull the cord out of the jack.

I head into the bedroom, blow out the candle and lie there staring into the dark. Where can I get a job? There must be someplace in town. If I'm working, how do I take care of the place? What am I going to do?

There's a truck chasing me. Justin is trying to run me down. I can't escape. I jerk awake, roll over and cry. It doesn't matter anymore why he lied. He stole my life from me. He didn't ask. He didn't talk to me first. He just took it.

Day 20 Trouble Is Coming

Dawn drags me out of bed. I slept, but don't feel like it. Sassy isn't on the bed and the sheets are a twisted mess. Maybe I'll change them this morning. These do look really dirty. I feel dirty. My clothes are dirty. Even the underwear I keep rinsing out feels dirty.

Coffee wakes me up. Being broke breaks over me. I can't even summon up anger at Justin to fill the void. "I'm scared, Sassy. I'm really scared. What are we going to do? How do I pay for things we need?"

The phone sits in its cradle. If I plug it in, it's working. I still don't want to talk to Justin. The cord remains draped over the phone.

Routine takes me to the barn. Not even having Precious kick the bucket sloshing milk out excites me. The sunrise comes and goes. I don't see it. Arlo gets the milk. I forget to keep any for the house so the oatmeal is dry, no milk, no jelly, no raisins. And I can't buy any.

When the goats and I walk to the driveway gate, the new cows are still in the hay field. Maybe I can put the others in with them. Maybe tomorrow. Their owner better come get them. I won't be here. Sassy and I will be living in my truck somewhere. Maybe I can be a nomad moving around hiring out to clear land with my goats.

Looking at the last section of fence I find I'm only half a dozen posts from done. "This is a waste of my time. I have to sell. The next owners won't care." I turn to walk away. There's nothing at the house. I turn back and start straightening posts. Lunch time finds this section done.

"Where to now? I think I'll do that other end. The cows can come back in here once that end is up. If they're still here." I pick up the tools. The sledge hammer feels so heavy. I let it drag across the pasture.

Unmistakable whomping announces the helicopter. I drop the tools by the fence and wait. It settles onto the pasture.

"How's it going?" asks Mike.

I burst into tears. Mike shifts uneasily from foot to foot. "Sorry," I choke out. "The phone's working. My louse of a husband took all my money. I'm broke. I can't pay you for the groceries, if you brought any."

"FEMA sent the food. They even had some cat and dog food. I think I saw a dog here over with the goats."

"That's Arlo, my guard dog. And he's almost out of food too. Thanks."

"There's a couple of men cutting the trees across your road."

"Big, black pickup?"

"Yes."

"Justin."

"Your husband? I wondered who it was. They'll have the trees cleared in a couple of days, cleared enough you can get to town."

"Won't do me any good. I can't pay for anything, no food, no feed. And he won't."

"Check with the FEMA office. They may be able to help you."

"I need a job."

"You drove a truck?"

"Yes. Justin wants me to drive again. I don't want to go on the road again."

"There's a service in town, takes people shopping, to doctor's appointments and stuff. They hire a lot of drivers."

"Maybe they'll hire me. Thanks. I didn't know about them." A job prospect lightens my mood.

"Well, I brought out groceries. Can you get them to the house from here?"

"I'll take the tractor back. I can pile them on it."

"Great. I'll start unloading them. You should be able to get out of here, but I'll check next week to be sure, if you don't let the office know."

"You've been a lot of help. I wouldn't have made it through without the water and stuff."

"It's great to hear that. So many people gripe we don't do enough."

There are two boxes. I see flour, sugar, oatmeal, powdered milk. I laugh. "Hey, Mike, why don't you give the milk to someone who needs it?"

"I just deliver. The boxes are all alike."

After the helicopter leaves, I go for the tractor. Even Justin coming my way can't erase my elation at thinking I can go to town in a few days. I'll look up that place and apply for a job. There must be other places needing drivers for around town.

I chug my way back to the house on the tractor with jugs of water and boxes of food piled on the tray over the forks. The supplies are dropped off on my way to the tractor shed. The tractor is parked again. I won't need it until I start the hay field and do the long fence along the road.

"Sassy, you are saved. Mike brought cat kibble." I stash the jugs of water. A gallon doesn't go very far. "I need the electricity back on. Running water, plenty of it, would be a dream come true. I'll have to go to the laundromat and wash clothes. All that takes is money. I must have some change around."

The boxes of food are unloaded. The bag of dog food will last Arlo a few days. He's a big dog and eats a lot.

A loaf of bread is in one box along with peanut butter and jelly. Both of those are in large containers. The jelly won't last long without the refrigerator, so I'm generous with it on the sandwich. Once Justin clears the road, maybe the electric crew will get the power on.

"If Justin is cutting trees, he bought another chainsaw. The other one is here. How did he pay for it? Did he charge it on the credit card?"

The last of my sandwich goes down as I head for the phone. Anything on that credit card will be left for me to pay. I'm sure of that. "Justin won't pay it off. I need to stop more charges on it." I dial the bank and go through the identification routine. "I need to put a freeze on my credit card. Can I do that now? Can you tell me how much is charged on it for this month?"

When I hang up, I know Justin charged the chainsaw and supplies for it. And there's a motel charge. That hundred dollars left in the savings account may not cover even the minimum payment. "I am in trouble." I pull the plug again.

On my way back to the cow pasture, I stop to stare down the road. Even if the trees are cut and moved the road is barely passable. It's full of ruts like the ones I filled to get the tractor across. I wonder what Justin is doing about them.

"Mike said I have a couple of days until he gets here. Do I stay here and talk to him? I could move my truck down on the road by the pasture and take off for town when he pulls in the driveway. But what would he do while I'm not here? I better stay."

Justin isn't the road crew. He can't get in, I can't get out over the ditches along the other culvert. Debris isn't gravel, but it seems to work. I start hauling debris off the hay field fence and dumping it in the ditches.

"Justin, what a surprise. I didn't think you were coming back. Care to explain those secret bank accounts?" Dump.

"A new chainsaw? Are you paying for this one? That will be a first." Dump.

"When are you giving my money back to me? It is my money. You never put a cent into the so-called joint account or this place. You're a liar and a thief." Dump.

"Sell? Don't think so. Drive? With you? Never!" Dump.

These ditches take seven stretches of fence debris. I jump up and down on the piles. They seem firm enough to drive over. I stare down the road. There aren't enough trees between me and Justin. He'll be here too soon. I'm scared.

It's only mid-afternoon. I walk back to the cow pasture to tackle this fence. I start at the gate in the center working my way back to the corner. I should be at the corner able to hear him coming when he gets here.

The goats and chickens stay on short rations. I don't have a job yet. I'm still broke, more than broke, in debt. Justin took the money. He's not going to give it back. I don't want to owe Lee for feed unless I can pay him. I wonder if my milk and egg customers will still want the milk and eggs. I'll have to call them later.

In the house I light one of my remaining candles. How am I going to buy more? If the electricity comes back on, how do I pay that bill?

Macaroni and cheese are on the menu tonight. I might prefer broccoli, but the can contains peas. Afterwards I settle into my recliner. The Oregon Trail beckons, but I can't concentrate. And I want to save the candle for tomorrow.

All night I fall asleep only to jerk awake from nightmares. Justin is coming in two days. Rather, he will be here tomorrow. What am I going to do? What can I do? And underneath I know that is why he took the money. Does he really think I will just do as he tells me? Will I? That's what I've always done.

My eyes are open. My body is tired, but my mind won't shut off. I wish I could sit up and read. But there are no lights and only a few candles. Tears roll down my cheeks tickling my neck as they gather to drop to the pillow.

Day 21 Indecision and Fear

I must have gone back to sleep as the dark is now gray. My muscles ache. My mind is leaden repeating the mantra Justin is coming over and over.

Coffee helps lift the brain to fog. Maybe I should crawl back in bed after chores. A repeat of the other day would not be good.

At every break during milking, I have to resist the urge to curl up. All I want to do is hide under a blanket, make time stand still, send Justin back to St. Louis, even have the flood back. "What am I going to do?"

After milking, I try going back to bed. "This is stupid. I'm not sleepy. All I'm doing is making up things about seeing Justin tomorrow. I need to fix that fence."

The debris is off eight stretches of the fence. I collect the come-along and sledge hammer from the cow barn to straighten posts. This takes total concentration so I try to shut out any thoughts about Justin or tomorrow. One by one the posts get put back in place.

When I've worked on six posts, I stop and start on the debris. "I have to remember he's a liar, a thief. Even if he explains, that doesn't change a thing. I'm not going back to St. Louis with him. I'm not going to drive a truck with him. He can go back to St. Louis and never come back here again."

My back screams for a halt after eight more sections. I straighten up staring down the road. Shudders crawl up my spine. Justin will be mad. It's habit to obey, to avoid his anger. "What am I going to do?" Tears gather in the corners of my eyes.

I know it's lunch time. There's a knot where my stomach should be. Hunger dances around the fringes. My shoulders keep hunching around as I walk back to the house. I shiver in the August heat.

Back in the house I put water on to heat. Coffee, hot coffee will melt that cold. Not too hot, my tongue reminds me.

I stare at my cookbook. "Is there a safer place to hide those papers? A drawer? He'll look. No, the cookbook is a good place."

Warmth does seep out from the coffee. The knot in my stomach eases. My hands relax wrapped around my mug. "I can do this. I can face Justin. If I can do the work around here, I can stay here. I'll find a job." The words sound good, but ring hollow in my ears.

My sandwich is drippy as the peanut butter and jelly are slathered on. I'm glad I washed my hands off at the rain barrel on the way into the house as I am now licking jelly off my hands. It's safer to go outside with this sandwich, so I do.

Standing out in the yard I look around. There are the trees to cut up. I'll need a smaller chainsaw, one I can handle. Chainsaws are not cheap and I already owe for this new one Justin bought. At least he can't charge anything else on my card.

A sudden smile curves my lips. Justin will get a big surprise the next time he tries to use that card. I did make sure he couldn't cancel the freeze when I talked to the bank.

And Justin is doing me a favor. He's clearing the road so I can get to town. I'll get his name taken off the card when I get to town. And I'll see what I have to do to get his name off the property deed. I paid for this place and it is mine!

A couple of handfuls of water out of the rain barrel get the sticky feel off my hands. The fence is waiting. I straighten my shoulders. I've fixed over half the cow pasture fence on my own. I can face Justin and tell him to leave. I can do it.

By milking time, all my doubts have come back. My muscles are tense, stiff. I'm cold inside.

"Precious, what am I going to do? What will happen to us? He stole all our money."

I hug my goat's neck wetting it with tears. "What will happen to you?"

Precious and Priscilla are anxious to get back in the barn. Goats do not like being hugged. I know this, but I need a hug right now.

"Topaz, we'll know by tomorrow night. He'll be here by then. What am I going to do? I need to be brave. I'm not brave. I'm scared."

Then Gem and Jewel are on the stands. "You are so lucky. You aren't worried about tomorrow. It's up to me. And I'm worried."

There's another box of macaroni and cheese in the food box Mike brought. I don't like the processed cheese much, too intense, but I fix it anyway. Even this comfort food doesn't help.

Forget reading. I sit hugging Sassy until she struggles to get loose. Then I sit hugging my knees to my chest trying not to think about tomorrow.

Bed has no appeal, but I blow out the candle and shuffle my way into the bedroom. My clothes slip onto the floor and I slide in under the sheet. I'm cold and add the blanket throwing them over my head. I shiver, shut my eyes and pretend to sleep.

The clock ticks. I concentrate on the ticks, counting them, letting the sound fill my mind. Until I don't hear the ticking anymore.

Day 22 Justin

It's still dark. I stare toward the window. Not even a glimmer of light shows. Every muscle is tense. I know it's too early to get up. Staring at the window doesn't bring sleep back. Only terrible thoughts of what might happen when Justin gets here fill my brain.

Determined to go back to sleep, I close my eyes. From my neck down I force my muscles to relax, my mind on relaxing them. By the time I get down to my toes, some of the tension is gone. A second round lessens it more. The third begins.

Light is streaming in my window. Tossing off the sheet, I throw on my clothes. Lighting the stove, I find my hands are trembling slightly. Hot coffee radiates warmth through me, but not courage. I head out to the barn.

My mind is blank. What am I doing? Chickens. The chickens need feed, water and their door opened. I get the bucket of feed and walk over to the chicken house. The chickens are out in the yard. I forgot to close their door last night.

"One, two, three." It's hard to count the hens as they move around, but all of them seem to be there. No pile of feathers is at their door or in their house. "That was lucky. I guess the raccoons were busy elsewhere."

Back in the milk room I dump full rations in the dishes. The goats have no objections. It dawns on me when I have to wait for Gem to finish eating. Does it matter? Will we still be here in a week?

"Take milk back for breakfast." Most of the milk is in Arlo's dish before I remember again. There is enough left in the bucket for oatmeal.

The oatmeal boils over on the stove. I was staring out the window, but don't know what I was looking at. I look at the papers in my cookbook. Should I add others? These should be enough. I put them back. Will they be safe here? Where is safe?

Sassy meows at me. "Didn't I feed you?" Her bowl is empty. I put kibble in it.

Maybe I will stay in the house and read. No, I'll work on the fence. Maybe he won't get here today.

The goats are waiting for me at the driveway gate. I open it and stand staring up the road. Do I hear a chainsaw? Voices? Nothing. I close the gate and walk to the cow pasture.

Every time I face down the road, I stop and listen. The wire gets cleared. The posts get pulled up and tapped into place. And the road stays empty.

Lunch time is announced by my stomach. I walk up the road, back up the driveway and keep staring down the road. Faint sounds come up the road. Chainsaw? Wind? Imagination?

Lunch uses more bread. Maybe I'll make French toast for dinner. Lots of jelly on the bread as I know it will start molding in another day or two. What will I say when Justin gets here? will he let me say anything? I'm afraid of what he will do and say. "Time stand still. I want more days just fixing fence, no complications."

When I get back to the driveway gate, there's no doubt. I hear a chainsaw. There must be another tree down below the one I see as no one is at that tree yet. My hands cover my face as my body shivers.

A deep breath steadies me. I go back to straightening posts. Eight posts remain before I get to the corner. The trees are spaced apart enough I can see the tree at the end of the hay field.

Six posts were done before lunch. Another six are straight before I see the first branches on that tree begin to fall. I finish the last two posts to complete this section. The tools go back in the cow barn.

Should I go down to the tree? I'll wait. I start moving debris off the hay field wire working my way down from the corner. Each armload off, I stand up and look down the road.

I'd looked at that tree. It is one big tree. The trunk is close to two feet thick. The chainsaw roars as it cuts through. Maybe I should take the tractor down to help move the pieces off the road. That will take me down to Justin and I'm not ready yet. I wonder if any of the other trees were that big and how he moved those pieces.

My back insists on stopping. I walk back to the driveway. I'll take the tractor and chain down. I can help move those big pieces. My hands are shaking as I put the chain on the tractor, start it and back out of its shed.

Every turn of the tires takes me closer to that tree and Justin. I want to turn around, go back to the house. I can't. And I'm at the tree, turning around to back up to the huge pieces of trunk.

"What do you think you are doing? Get off that tractor." Justin grabs my arm and pulls me down on the road. "Took your sweet time getting here. We've been working four days cutting up trees to get here. You didn't even cut the branches on this tree. There's a chainsaw. Why didn't you use it?"

"It's too big and heavy."

"Expecting me to come rescue you more likely. This place is a waste of time, money and work. Look at those fences. Who's going to fix them? Not me! You? Don't make me laugh. What have you been doing? Sitting around in the house waiting for the fences to fix themselves?"

By now Justin is shouting at me. I cower under the noise. All my anger, my fear dives into hiding from the onslaught.

"Don't have anything to say? Good. We'll take care of this. You get back to the house and pack. By the time we get to the house, you better be ready to leave. We have to be in St. Louis Tuesday to pick up a load. You will go with me as my partner."

I stare at Justin. St. Louis Tuesday? What is he talking about?

"I told the company you were teaming up with me after I got you. They gave me time because of the flood. Now get up there and pack."

"The animals," I mumble.

"This place is history. Jeremy will take care of things here. You are leaving with me. Now get going!"

I don't want to go. No. I won't go. That's what I should say. I don't.

"What are you waiting for? Get out of my way! You better be ready to leave when we get to the house. Move!"

Habit turns me toward the house. Habit carries me back in the house. A wife does what her husband tells her to do. I take down my duffle, unzip it and open my dresser drawers. Sassy jumps in one. I pick her up and hug her tight.

There in the closet sits that briefcase. Justin will take it. It will vanish. He's my husband. I put Sassy down to pack my duffle. Jeremy can pack my things and put them in storage. Maybe I can get them out sometime in the future. Maybe Justin will let me keep Sassy with us. He put up with that dog and Sassy is a lot less trouble.

Underwear. Jeans. Shirts. Brush. Bathroom items. The duffle doesn't hold enough. Surely I can have a small suitcase too? Didn't I used to have one, before moving here?

The small suitcase is in the back of the closet. I get it out and start packing it too. I zip up my duffle and close the suitcase. I'll need to get Sassy's litter pan, litter, dishes, kibble. Justin won't make me leave her behind, will he?

In the kitchen I reach for my cookbook to get the papers. Justin lied. He stole money from me. Now he's trying to steal my home. "What am I doing? I'm not leaving. I'm not his partner." The papers go back in the cookbook and onto the shelf. The duffle gets thrown into the closet. The suitcase gets shoved in after it. My keys go into my pocket. Maybe I'll go into town, talk to the bank. Maybe I can get a loan, a mortgage to get me by until I find a job.

"Don't worry, Sassy. I'm not leaving. This is our home."

I walk back to the top of the driveway to watch the action down the road. Justin is using the tractor to pull a length of trunk around to lie along the road. Branches are moving onto piles along the road. Who is this Jeremy? And what does Justin think he will take care of? Irritation nudges me.

A second piece of trunk gets pulled over to the side of the road. What will happen to them? Someone may want them for firewood. The goats would enjoy all those leaves on the branches. Maybe I'll take them down there tomorrow and do some work on the hay field fence.

"Look at those fences? Waiting for me to fix them?" I mimic. "Liar, look at the cow pasture fences. I fixed them. I can fix the hay pasture fences."

The tractor is coming up the road now. I wait before swinging the gate open. The cows have moved over near the creek, away from all the commotion. I still don't want to give them an opportunity to come back into the yard.

Justin drives by taking the tractor back into the shed. He parks, gets off leaving the key in the ignition. Why? We never leave the key there. I go in and get the key.

"Leave it. Jeremy will need to know where it is when he sells the thing."

I walk out of the shed with the key.

Neither of us speaks as Justin is already going back down the driveway and down the road. He is angry. I'm not. I should be. I'm numb. Even fear has left.

Some time later Justin drives down the road and up the driveway. He and Jeremy get out. Jeremy walks around staring at everything.

Justin stomps over. "Are you packed?"

"No. I'm not leaving."

"Listen, Mindy, you are my wife. I just spent four days cutting up trees to get here for you. I'm hot and tired and in a hurry. You will do as I tell you. Now, either you pack or I will pack for you. We are leaving in an hour. I need to show Jeremy around and tell him what to do. Get in the house and pack."

"No. I'll show Jeremy around my place. Then the two of you can leave. Thanks for clearing the road."

"Move!" Justin grabs my arm and pulls me to the house. He shoves me in the door. "You have an hour. Get moving."

"I have to milk."

"You have to pack." Justin turns and walks toward Jeremy, stops and comes back. "Where are the keys to the truck?"

"Why?"

"I sold it to Jeremy."

"You can't do that. It's my truck. I bought it. I paid for it. I'm not selling it."

"It's sold. Give me the keys."

"No."

Justin storms past me and starts pulling drawers open, checking counters. "Where are the keys?" He looks at me and sees a bulge in my pocket. He grabs me, shoves his hand into my pocket to pull out my keys. I grab them and hang on. He slaps me, yanks them out of my hand and walks out of the house. "Get packed."

I walk back into the bedroom. My cheek stings. Justin hit me. I know he's angry, but he hit me. I'm crying. He sold my truck. He stole my money. He lied to me. He hit me! I sink onto the bed and cry.

Later the two come into the house. "There's a cat somewhere. You can take it to the shelter or leave it to fend for itself. Use it for target practice. I don't care which. There's a livestock auction in town. If you call, they have people to pick animals up. You can sell the goats and cows there. The dog too, probably. You keep half the money, give the rest to me. Do whatever you want with the things in the house, furniture and stuff. Sell the tractor."

He's selling my things and taking the money. The tears stop. He's leaving Sassy to starve or worse. He's sending the goats and steers to the auction. What about the cows that aren't mine? Is he selling them too?

Anger curls up inside me. I try to control it. I have to control it or I can't think straight. It turns cold. I march out to the front room. "This is my house, my property, my belongings. You can't sell my things. I'm not selling my things."

"Why not? I helped pay for them."

"Liar. You're nothing but a liar and a thief. You never put a dime into this place. You've been lying to me for years about it. I saw the statements. You and your private bank account, your private investment account. Jeremy, that is my truck. Give me back my keys! Then both of you get out of my house, off my property or I'll call the sheriff."

Justin shoves past me and into the bedroom. He comes back out with the briefcase and takes it out to his truck. When he comes back in, he stomps over to me.

"That is my briefcase. You had no right to open it. What did you do with the truck title? What else did you take?"

"It's my truck and it's not for sale."

"Fine. We'll play your little game. Jeremy, I'll have to get a title. It shouldn't take long. A bill of sale should be enough until the new title comes and I send it to you. We'll stay the night and I can stop at the license office in the morning before we head to St. Louis."

"I'm not going to St. Louis. This is my home and I'm not leaving. Both of you are leaving. You go back to St. Louis. Alone!"

"We are going to St. Louis. You are my wife and will do what I tell you. Everything you have, every penny you earn is mine."

"I'm not your property. I earned that money. Those are my things. You didn't pay for them. I did. This is my house. Get out!"

"That power of attorney gives me the right to do whatever I want with this property and everything on it. And I'm selling it. Are you packing? Or do I pack for you? I'm sure that title is around here. I will find it. Then we are leaving."

Justin starts pulling drawers open. Contents hit the floor as he paws through them. Jeremy is backing toward the door.

"Stop it!" I slam the next drawer closed. "You can drag me off, but you can't make me drive again. Why would I ever want to drive with a liar and a thief?"

Justin grabs my arm hard. I wince. He throws me across the room and yanks the drawer out spilling the contents onto the floor.

I spin toward Jeremy. "Oh, Jeremy, if you sell all those cows, you go to jail for rustling. Most of them showed up during and after the flood and belong to a neighbor. I left word for him so he knows they're here."

"Jail? You're kidding, right? They couldn't put me in jail, if I didn't know, could they? I'd lose my license."

"I guess you'll find out."

"Hey, Justin, this isn't what I agreed to. I'm not going to jail for you. You said she wanted to leave."

"You agreed to sell the place. You took the truck."

"That was before. You said she wanted to leave. You said it would be easy, just sell the stuff, list the place."

"She's leaving with me, just like I said. Find out who the cows belong to, sell the others. Nothing's changed."

"Hey, Jeremy, know how to milk? My goats have to be milked. If you don't, they could die before being sold."

"That's not true, is it? Justin?"

"Know anything about chickens? Raccoons love chicken dinner. You don't keep them locked up, you won't have any to sell."

"Shut up!" yells Justin. "Jeremy, don't listen to her. You do what I told you, what we agreed on."

"No. Enough. I don't need any trouble with the law. I don't know anything about goats or chickens or finding cow owners." Jeremy tosses me the keys. "I'm out of here. You can drive me to town."

We watch Jeremy leave. The screen slams shut behind him. The truck door slams.

Justin looks down at me, hands balling up, starts forward raising a fist. I cringe and back up. His hands tremble. His red face distorts.

"You hit me and I'll call the sheriff. How will your company like it if you're charged with beating your wife?"

I can hear all the names he'd like to call me, all the things he'd like to do to me. "I'll call the sheriff and I'll press charges." He stops.

"This is your last chance." Justin storms into the bedroom. He finds the duffle and suitcase. "Well, look here. You packed. That's a good wife. Now, let's go out and get in the truck. I'll talk to Jeremy. He'll stay."

"No, I'll stay. Put those down." I snag the duffle and throw it back in the bedroom. Justin hangs onto the suitcase, the center of a tug of war. The lock opens spilling my things onto the floor. He lets go and I sprawl on the floor. The suitcase slams into my side from his kick.

"You'll lose your precious job, if you go to jail."

123

Justin stares down at me. "The account is empty. I won't pay the credit card. I won't send you any money. I will blacklist you as a driver. No company will touch you, after I get done. You want to sit out here on this sorry place? You do it with nothing."

"Answer me one thing. Why did you lie? You made such a big deal out of starting that joint account. Were you planning to steal my money even then?"

"I didn't steal your money. It belongs to me. You are my wife." Justin glares at me, turns away to stomp toward the door.

"Why did you lie to me? Why'd you marry me? Was it all money? I mean, you had those accounts from the beginning."

Justin looks at me. "We could've been rich. We made a good team. We were making money. My investments were making money. You really thought I would throw that away on this sorry place? You had to play homesteader. I thought you'd get tired of it in a couple of years. I knew the place was a dud when you bought it. That's why she sold it so cheap. You are such a fool. I don't need you. I have to get back to St. Louis." He slams the screen door to the mud porch open, then the porch door. The doors slam shut. The truck door slams. The engine roars to life.

Justin turns his truck around, gunning the motor to spray mud and gravel as he drives to the road and turns toward town. He's gone. The money's gone with him. I walk to the top of the driveway to close the gate. I won. I'm still here. The place is mine.

And it hits me. "Now what? The credit card bill is hundreds of dollars. There's nothing in the account. I need feed, food, a job." Back in the house I curl up in my recliner hugging Sassy. "You're safe. He was going to leave you out here alone." She purrs and curls up on me to sleep. I cry.

It's close to dark when I look up. "Chores! The goats!"

Grabbing the milk pail, I race out to let the goats back in the yard. They race up to the safety of their barn as though pursued. I follow.

The chickens are in their house so I lock up. Forget the feed tonight. The goats are eager to come in for grain and milking even with strange shadows on the walls from the flashlight. Arlo gets most of the milk.

French toast makes a comforting dinner. I call my egg customers. That money will cover the laundromat. Tomorrow night I will have clean clothes. I need the refrigerator working for the milk.

The drawers get picked up and replaced. The contents get dumped back in. Sorting is easier with more light than my one candle.

Later I crawl into bed huddling under a blanket, Sassy curled up against me. Waves of fear and joy take turns in my mind. Joy wins out with a decision to sell two steers.

Day 23 New Reality

Light creeps up lighting the hill I see out my window. It's time to get up. My eyes close as I savor the warmth in my nest under the blanket. Sassy stretches, sniffs my nose, curls up and waits for me to move.

"Town! I can go to town today." I sit up rolling my cat over. "Hey, Sassy, I can see people, get my mail, go to the library and check email. There's the bank and job hunting. Maybe I should find a lawyer. Justin won't take me back now, even if I wanted him back."

Up and dressed, I know I need a bath and clean clothes. There are clothes in the closet and I'll use some rainwater from a barrel to wash off. "Laundry. I'll need money for the laundromat. Remember to take eggs. And call the livestock auction about the steers."

I look at the coffeemaker in the kitchen. The expresso stuff is drinkable. Real coffee would be nice. Maybe I can let the electric company know the road is open. Maybe I should wait until I've tried going to town on it first.

The goats dawdle over their grain, or so it seems. They keep looking at me between bites. I can't stand still and pace the room.

When is the auction? I need to sell those steers so I can buy feed. I'll have to run a feed bill today. But the goats and chickens are safe. No sale barn for them. No groceries for me. Can I get another box of food from FEMA? Should I take bottles to get water?

Stepping out on the porch, I take some deep breaths. "Calm down. Town will be there. Look at that sunrise."

The colors have faded. The few puffy, scattered clouds blaze a blinding white. Rays of sunlight pierce the trees topping the hill. The sky fades from a deep blue to the pale blue of a summer sky.

Gem calls from inside. I go back to let her down. The herd ignores the hay in the trough. They want to go out to the creek for the day. "I'm not going to be home, girls. Maybe you should stay in." They don't think so. I leave the gate closed for now.

The chickens too think I should open their gate and let them run. "You should be safe enough. Maybe I'll wait until I'm ready to leave. It is still early."

It takes time to cook oatmeal on the stove. This morning I wish the microwave worked. Electricity is so convenient, so normal.

Eating breakfast a bite at a time, I find a piece of paper and a pen. "I better have a list today. Let's see. First, the post office and the mail. Next, deliver eggs, then I can go to the laundromat. Take the water jugs. Find a lawyer. Take the papers. Go to the library. Take the books."

The list takes both sides of the paper. "I'll never get all of this done today. I have to get home in time to milk." I finish, wash the bowl and start getting things together to go to town. A phone call to the livestock barn arranges for someone to get the two steers the morning of the next sale a week from now as the sale was yesterday. I'll have to get them back in the cow pasture before that.

"I almost lost you," I tell my truck as I settle into the driver's seat. "Justin was going to give you away. He did give you away. You're mine now. Let's go to town."

Justin and Jeremy did a good job cutting up the trees and piling brush out of the way. There's just enough room for my truck to get through. The road is another matter. Ruts, ditches, potholes keep me barely moving trying not to bounce the truck apart. The seven miles takes almost an hour.

Once I get onto the pavement, the road is better. Even that has lots of potholes and washed out places. Trees are down and the sound of chainsaws is common.

Once I get into town, things look almost normal along the main road except for big piles of brush and branches. Looking down from intersections, side roads still have trees and brush and big potholes. I start down my list.

By the time I get home, a bit late as it takes so long on the gravel road, I have a lawyer looking into a divorce settlement, clean clothes, a pile of mail, jugs of water, a box of food from FEMA, sacks of feed and new books to read. I took some of the money out of the account to get a propane lantern for light. I put in job applications and hope to hear soon.

The credit cards need to be paid off, but I'll worry about that later. Justin will pay me back, the lawyer assures me, especially since I have proof of his secret accounts. Life is looking up.

At the house I settle back into the new and old routine. I am home. And it is my home.

Epilogue

It's been a busy month since Justin stormed off.

I finished getting the cow pasture fence back up. The scoop wasn't too hard to attach to the tractor to clean out the oxbow so there was water for the steers again. The cows and steers eagerly followed a line of range cubes back across the road.

Two steers went to the auction. That gave me s little money, enough to pay the credit card minimum, pay the feed bill and get more plus some groceries.

The goats busily explored their hill pasture finding branches and trees down to supply them with leaves except they were pretty wilted. The pasture was eaten down by the cows. When I work on the fences, I let them out to eat along the road and creek.

When the neighbor showed up about his cows, I was surprised. He's near my age, divorced and working which is why he didn't have time to get the cows off the pasture before the flood. It cost him as only a third of the cows had showed up at my place. He arranged to pay rent for them until the end of September and has started dropping by with his son on weekends. I am putting the hay field fence back up and had the oxbow there dug out, so they have a place to stay and the money is welcome.

In fact, I was working on that fence when the road crew finally came down to finish clearing and fixing the road. Other people, probably from a saw mill, had already come by to pick up the logs along the road.

Having the road cleared and graded makes getting to work much easier. Yes, I'm driving for the transportation company three days a week. They needed someone for their long trips to Springfield, Columbia and St. Louis so I make a run to each one every week with people needing to get to doctor's appointments. It doesn't pay a lot, but does cover my main bills.

Justin got a notice from my lawyer to give my money back plus or find me after half his assets. It took a few months, but he transferred seventy thousand dollars into the account. I transferred it to a new account, one in my name only and paid off the credit card. He signed the property over to me along with the tractor and my truck and signed divorce papers.

On a whim I stopped by the real estate office one day and asked about the property next door. It wasn't listed for sale anywhere. An older woman broke in. "That old place. The widow is in the nursing home. Her children want her to sell the place. She wants one of them to live there and is upset none of them want to."

"What's her name?"

"Lilian McElroy."

"I think I'll have a talk with Mrs. McElroy. Her children may not want the place, but I'm interested."

"We'll be glad to handle the paperwork, if she sells."

"Thanks."

When I meet her, Lilian McElroy reminds me of Mrs. Watson. She's full of stories about the old place. I tell her about my place and she remembers when the Watsons moved there.

By the time I leave, she's planning to sell the place to me for much less than it's probably worth even though it is run down, the fields grown up. It will mean paying a mortgage off and a lot of work. But I'll have pastures to raise cattle, a real cow calf operation. And it will be big enough to pay its way.

That afternoon I walk down the road, around the gate posts, down the driveway to the old house. Standing by the porch steps I look out over the place and see it the way Mrs. McElroy described it. I want it to look that way again.

The house could be fixed up and rented, maybe. There may be a market for someplace far out of town. The metal roof is dented, but in good shape. It does need insulation under it to deaden the noise of rain hitting it. I'll have to hire help.

For some reason my neighbor comes to mind. He's trying to be a cattle baron too, but has to work full time. He might be interested in being a partner. He is good looking and good company. Not that I'm looking for romance, strictly business.

Walking back home I laugh at myself. I'm dreaming of being a cattle baron, like in an old western movie. In truth, I just want a quiet life, maybe a husband who loves being out like I do, a couple of children.

For now, I have my house, snug and safe in storms, my Sassy and my goats. That is the life I want.

Author's Notes

Thank you for choosing my novel to read. If you enjoyed it, please let others know about it. Leaving a review would help others find this book. You can find out more about me and my other books at my website: www.goatkeeperspress.com.

I read and review a wide variety of books on GoodReads.

The ideas for this book came from many places. One was the changing climate with more major storms occurring dropping larger amounts of rain in many places around the world. Such a storm did come by my part of the Ozarks.

This storm was called a derecho. Our creek rose five feet in half an hour. Falling trees took out three electric poles. Unlike the storm in this novel, ours lasted only a few hours. The damage on the hills can still be seen.

Mindy and Justin are composites of people I have known or known of over the years. Women have struggled against cultural attitudes placing them closer to being the property of their husbands rather than companions or partners for centuries. This attitude seems more deeply rooted in very conservative and religious areas like the Ozarks.

I have lived as a homesteader in the Ozarks for thirty years. Floods have washed out the road and fences, not on the scale of the novel, but close enough for me to know the effects. Even as I wrote the novel, our electricity went out for close to twenty-four hours giving me a reminder of what happens to refrigerator and freezer. This outage wasn't storm related, but due to an animal shorting out a substation.

Even the phone problem was one I had encountered as our lines are buried with posts at intervals. One post had the lid knocked off so rain got inside. It took two months of off and on phone problems before the technician found the problem.

People living in cities, and I was one many years ago, have their own sets of problems. They seem often to think rural people don't have such problems. Perhaps many of the city problems don't plague rural areas, but there is another set to cope with.

And I do keep several jars filled with water in case the electricity goes out so our water pump doesn't work. Rain barrels are at every corner of the house. There was even a time many years ago when a rainstorm became a shower for me.

Other Books by Karen GoatKeeper

Fiction

Broken Promises, Hazel Whitmore #1 introduces Hazel as her life collapses leaving her dealing with her father's death, bullying at school, loss of friends and moving.

Old Promises, Hazel Whitmore #2 follows Hazel to her new home in rural Crooked Creek, Missouri. She must adjust to no cellphone or internet, no friends and dealing with a family feud with relatives she has just met.

Mistaken Promises, Hazel Whitmore #3 finds the feud Hazel thought was over, isn't. Someone wants Hazel to pay for the past and tries time and time again to collect.

Dora's Story is the fictional biography of a dairy goat and her various owners. Each needs Dora. Most love her. Many are helped by her.

Capri Capers takes the reader on a wild melodramatic ride of cliff hangers and perils as dastardly villains try to steal some of Harriet's new wealth.

Edwina appears to Aleta when she most needs a friend. The two seek a way for Aleta to adjust to her newly divorced parents and defend against school bullies.

Running the Roads is what Ridge loves to do with his new car. He dreams of being a road rally driver and practices daily, but drives into trouble.

For Love of Goats shows the fun side of goats through tongue twisters, short alliterative stories, short fiction and reminiscences.

Picture Book

Waiting For Fairies about a child going out to see the fairies come to a fairy ring and finding some of the Ozark night creatures.

Nonfiction

Exploring the Ozark Hills is contains 84 nature essays with photographs spanning an Ozark year.

My Ozark Home remembers twenty-five years on my Ozark hills through photographs and haikus.

Goat Games invites you to learn about goats through pencil puzzles, stories and trivia.

The Pumpkin Project, a science activity book, immerses you in the science of pumpkins through investigations, projects, puzzles and stories.

The City Water Project, a science activity book, explores water and where people get their water and what they do with it through investigations, activities, puzzles and stories.

Made in the USA
Monee, IL
22 August 2023

41460661R00075